DATE DUE		9/01
DEC 20 '01			
APR 10 03			
12-7-04			
JUL 21 '05			
8-26-15			
GAYLORD			PRINTED IN U.S.A.

Honor Bound

Also by Colleen Reece
in Large Print:

Alpine Meadows Nurse
Belated Follower
Come Home, Nurse Jenny
Everlasting Melody
The Heritage of Nurse O'Hara
The Hills of Hope
In Search of Twilight
Mysterious Monday
Nurse Autumn's Secret Love
Nurse Julie's Sacrifice
Trouble on Tuesday
Yellowstone Park Nurse

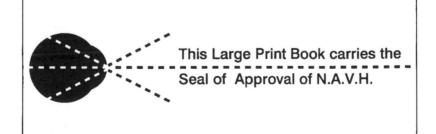

This Large Print Book carries the
Seal of Approval of N.A.V.H.

Honor Bound

Colleen Reece

Thorndike Press • Waterville, Maine

Published in 2001 by arrangement with
Colleen L. Reece.

Thorndike Press Large Print Christian Romance Series.

The tree indicium is a trademark of Thorndike Press.

The text of this Large Print edition is unabridged.
Other aspects of the book may vary from the original edition.

Set in 16 pt. Plantin by Al Chase.

Printed in the United States on permanent paper.

Library of Congress Cataloging-in-Publication Data
Reece, Colleen L.
   Honor bound / Colleen Reece.
     p. cm.
   ISBN 0-7862-3443-1 (lg. print : hc : alk. paper)
   1. Ranch life — Fiction. 2. Arizona — Fiction.
  3. Brothers — Fiction. 4. Large type books. I. Title.
  PS3568.E3646 H6 2001
  813'.54—dc21   2001027771

Honor Bound

1

The door to the playroom swung inward. Honor Brooks looked up from the table where she and five-year-old Heather had been making letters.

"Miss Brooks, Heather" — Ben Stone beamed as he looked down at his daughter and her governess — "how would you like to go to the Grand Canyon?"

Honor was speechless. Heather was not. "Daddy, Daddy!" She flung herself into her father's arms. "Are we really going?"

"We certainly are." Laurene Stone indolently posed in the doorway. "Since President Wilson signed it into a National Park it's really quite the place to go." Her usually petulant face showed a spark of interest. "I understand El Tovar Hotel is sumptuous. Several of my friends are going for the summer, and Ben needs time away from his law practice." Her cool eyes were almost fond as they swept over gray-clad Honor. "It will be good for you, too. You can take Heather out in the fresh air and sunshine."

"That's very kind of you." Honor blushed.

"It will take about a month to get ready.

7

I'll have all new clothing, of course. You're good with a needle, Honor. Would you like to remodel some of my present gowns for yourself?" A look of dismay crossed the carefully made-up face. "You weren't planning to go into mourning, were you?"

"Laurene!" Honor had never heard Ben Stone thunder before. Was this how he talked to lying witnesses in the court room?

Now Laurene had the grace to blush. "I didn't mean to be rude, or anything. It's just that at the Canyon and all — your brother wouldn't want you to wear black, would he? And being with Heather every day —"

Honor lost the rest of the explanation as a small hand slipped into hers. Heather stood with one finger in her mouth, her earlier joy of the news about their trip gone, showing clearly how the scene was affecting her.

"You're right, Mrs. Stone. Keith would never want me to wear black." She even managed a wan smile. "Your gowns are lovely, and I believe I can make suitable garments from them."

"There!" Laurene turned triumphantly to her husband. She pulled a bell rope and waited as a maid responded. "Sally, have Jimson bring down the trunk of clothes by my closet."

Heather crossed to her mother but looked

back at Honor, eyes still anxious. "They're really pretty. You'll look nice in them."

Honor forced herself to smile at Heather. "I'm sure I shall."

"Don't wear yourself out sewing, Miss Brooks."

The concern in her employer's voice unnerved Honor, but Sally was already draping gowns over every available chair — garnet satin, dark blue crepe, deep green, lovely amber — yards of gorgeous material trimmed with real lace. Some were far too decollete for Honor's taste, but they could be remodeled until even their original owner would not recognize them!

Last of all Laurene ordered Sally to open a satin-lined box.

"Oh!" Honor's dark blue eyes opened wide. Never had she seen such a beautiful frock. The white lace and satin were pearl-beaded — with even a small purse to match.

"You can get married in that one," Heather told her. The next instant her face clouded over. "You aren't going to get married and go away, are you?"

"Hardly." But Honor still fingered the frock, and a rich blush filled her face at the memory of a dark-haired soldier who had once briefly entered her life and then gone away.

When they had all left, Honor sat still, reliving another day when Ben Stone had entered the playroom. She had looked up that day, too — and the world had gone black as she saw the concern in her employer's face and the yellow telegram in his hand.

"Run along downstairs for a little while, please, Heather." He had waited as his daughter scampered out. "Miss Brooks — Honor —"

She had shoved back a lock of golden brown hair and a wave of faintness with one motion. "It's Keith, isn't it?"

Now she bit her lip, feeling the sickening taste of blood, trying to control her shaking hands. She resolutely clamped down the lid on memory of that day, as she had done dozens of times since. Keith was dead. She must go on.

You can't run away from it.

Had the words been whispered by her own heart, or were they merely the remains of the torture she had gone through these last weeks? Automatically her fingers lifted the heavy dresses, fitted them on hangers. One by one she carried them to her own room and placed them in the large wardrobe.

It was no use. All the gowns in the world could not stop her memories. She threw herself on the bed, letting the tears come. Would the pain never end?

There had been no trace of Ben Stone's usual courtroom crispness in his voice that day. But he had not attempted to soften the long-expected blow. "Yes. The War Department has confirmed his death." He had caught her as she swayed, helped her lean against the table. "He fell bravely, fighting for his country."

"That's comforting." Was that her own voice — bitter, harsh? "It's just that — all this time, when there was no word except he was missing — even since the war ended —" She could not go on.

"I know." Mr. Stone's face was sympathetic. "Evidently the War Department found someone who had actually seen Keith killed. There is no doubt." He cleared his throat. "They buried him in France, but if you want his body brought home, I'll see to it. And Honor, don't worry about expense. You've come to be part of our family. Everything will be taken care of."

Another tear fell, splashing against her clenched hands, as she remembered the kindness of the considerate employer for whom she had worked the past two years.

Thinking a walk would help, she tied a heavy hood over the bright brown hair so

11

like her brother Keith's. She caught back a cry of pain. It couldn't be possible Keith had died somewhere in France. When the Armistice Day bells rang on November 11, 1918, she had expected Keith home soon. He hadn't come. Months passed. A War Department telegram informed Honor, his only living relative, that Keith was missing in action.

A fresh wave of torture filled her as she remembered the long days, sleepless nights. Missing in action — dead or alive, no one knew. Yet deep inside was the assurance Keith would return. Surely God wouldn't let Keith die when he was all she had left!

Honor's face darkened. She couldn't think of God, not now. Snatching up a long cape that covered her dress to the hem, she wrapped it around her and fled into the early afternoon. She was unconscious of the stares from passersby. The long cloak was out of place in the late spring softness of San Francisco. Yet huddled in its depths Honor still felt cold, outside and inside.

Memories threatened to drown her: moving to Granny's cottage when both parents were killed in the great earthquake — she had been eleven, Keith six; teaching her little brother to read before he went to school; learning to rely on Granny for warmth and love.

Honor shuddered. Keith would answer her call no more. Why had he lied about his age to serve his country? Had God punished that lie with death on the battlefield? No! Her inner rebellion could not accept that. Keith had accepted Christ as his Savior when he was small. She could almost see his happy face becoming clouded over as he pleaded. "Honor, you have to accept Jesus, too. You have to be sorry for your sins and believe on the Lord."

She had scoffed in the lofty way her twelve years allowed. "If God really loved us, He wouldn't have let Mama and Daddy die."

Wisdom shone in the little boy's eyes. "The Bible says God loved us enough to send His own Son to die. God must have felt just as bad as we did about Mama and Daddy. Don't you listen when Granny tells us about Jesus and reads the verses?"

It hadn't been the last time Keith worried over her. Through their growing up years he kept on trying to win her to the Lord he loved. But Honor would not give up her stubbornness, even when Granny had died a few days before the Armistice. She clung to the idea Keith would be back. When he came would be time enough to talk about whether God loved her.

Her fingers clenched as a terrible thought crossed her mind: *If I'd accepted Christ, would Keith be alive now?*

No! Granny had taught them they were responsible for their own actions. God would hold them accountable for what they did — Honor's lips twisted — or for what they failed to do. Although others would be hurt by their actions, salvation was a one-to-one transaction between God and every person on earth.

Her remembrance left weakness. There had been an unpaid mortgage. The little home had been sold. The day had come when Honor's pocketbook and tiny cupboard in her dingy rented room were empty. She had tried to pray at first, but nothing got better. If God still knew she was alive, it didn't seem to matter to Him. Only the thought of Keith's homecoming had kept her moving down the street looking in every window for a HELP WANTED sign.

It was through an old family friend that Honor had met Ben Stone, a lawyer who wanted someone to give his four-year-old daughter the time and attention his wife was unable to give. Heather walked into the library of the Stones' mansion and into

14

Honor's heart at the same moment.

Laurene Stone seemed glad to be rid of even the minimal care she had been giving the child, and within a week Heather and Honor had become inseparable. The flaxen-haired little girl trotted after Honor eagerly and never argued when told to do something. Was it because of mutual loneliness? Laurene always seemed to have enough energy for balls and parties, but none for Heather. As a result, the child automatically turned to Honor's welcoming love. Honor believed that Mrs. Stone's only real problem was being spoiled, but she had little contact with her and poured out all the love she had on Heather.

Ben Stone had been as good as his word. It was several weeks before Keith's body could be shipped home, but Mr. Stone had done everything in his power to speed the process.

For Honor the waiting was even worse than when she had waited for Keith to come laughing in the door. Now her waiting was without hope. She was truly alone. Only Heather could reach through her suffering.

One night as she tucked the child in bed, Heather, rosy from splashing in the ornate marble tub, said, "I'm sorry your brother died. Daddy said he was a soldier." The beautiful face was wistful. "I never had a brother. Aren't you glad you did, even though he died?"

It caught Honor unprepared. Thoughts whirled through her feverish brain. Heather's face was turned up, expectantly waiting for an answer. What she said now might be of lasting value or damage to the child.

"Yes, Heather. I am glad I had a brother."

Heather's wide-open eyes indicated she was in the mood for confidences. "Tell me about him, when he was little like me."

Haltingly at first, then buoyed by her listener's interest, Honor uncovered some of the buried memories she had put aside because of their painfulness. It got easier as she went along. When Heather's reluctant eyelids finally stayed closed and Honor had slipped to her adjoining room, she lay awake for a time. It *was* better to remember, even painfully, than to try to forget. Heather's final sleepy comment still hung in the air. "I bet Keith'd be happy now he's gone to know you still have me."

A trickle of comfort touched her. It was true. She had a place to live, the love of Heather, admiration of Mr. Stone. She wasn't totally alone.

The child's love had helped her through

the hard memorial service, the final laying of Keith to rest in the sod of the country he loved and for which he had given his life. Yet in the weeks following the burial Honor was unable to pick up the shattered pieces and go on. She grew thin, pale, nervous. Even Heather wanted to know if she was sick. Honor told stories of her own childhood to amuse Heather and comfort herself, but continued to toss restlessly at night.

Alarmed, the Stones sent for a specialist, who checked her over. Honor overheard him tell them, "Shock. She carried on so long, but when hope was taken away, her body rebelled. She needs to get where there is a better climate. I don't like the sound of that cough she's developed."

Nothing more had been said until the Stones had come into the playroom today with the incredible announcement of a vacation to the Grand Canyon.

Honor suddenly realized she was chilly. Afternoon had given way to evening while she journeyed to the past. She hastily returned to the mansion and went in search of Heather.

The little girl was bubbling over with happiness. "Daddy says we're going in a great big car. There's going to be sand and mountains and all kinds of things to see! Aren't you excited, Honor?"

Honor led her small charge to the nursery, where Heather had her meals. "Of course I am. Keith —" her voice faltered, then firmly went on "— Keith and I always thought it would be a good place to visit."

With uncanny insight Heather read the meaning behind Honor's words. "Since your brother can't take you, we will. I heard Mama tell Daddy you needed to go —"

Honor's heart lifted. She wouldn't have thought Laurene cared about even a high-class servant that much. But Heather's continuing monologue shattered her illusions. "— and that we needed a vacation anyway, and this summer was the time to go while everyone thought it so smart."

Yet even those revelations could not completely dim Honor's anticipation. She lay in bed that night staring at the ceiling. She had always wanted to visit the Grand Canyon. She had read every book she could get her hands on, secretly hoping in her childish dreams she could visit a big cattle ranch someday, yet knowing the possibility was slight.

A rich blush crept up from the high ruffled neck of her cambric nightgown, touching her thin cheeks with color. She had even daydreamed of being mistress of such a ranch.

The excitement of the proposed exodus provided Honor with strength. Within a week she was working on the frocks Laurene had discarded. She and Heather took long walks past the great stores of the city, noting a knot of velvet here, a trick of gores there, that set apart the stylish frock from the ordinary. Honor's skillful needle faithfully transposed those tricks into her growing wardrobe. Heather learned to sew along with Honor's alterations, and doll clothes emerged for her favorites.

One evening Honor wore her new dark blue dress down to dinner. Most evenings she had dinner in the nursery with Heather, but on occasion she was pressed into service when an absent dinner guest made an uneven number. Her glowing cheeks were attractive and her eyes shone.

She wasn't prepared for Mrs. Stone's reaction. "Why, Honor, where did you get that lovely dress?" Astonishment narrowed Laurene's eyes. "That can't be —"

"It is." Honor laughed and whirled. "I wondered if you would recognize it."

"You certainly did a nice job!" Laurene peered at her more closely. "That fichu — it's just like the one on the Paris dress I found in a darling shoppe. If you don't mind, I may let you help me with my wardrobe at the canyon. I'd just as soon not bother with Sally."

"I'd be happy to help." Honor's sincere smile brought an answering glimmer to her employer's wife's eyes. Honor treasured the extra sign of friendliness. Laurene wasn't one to praise other women, especially one so insignificant as the governess.

It seemed only a few days passed, and suddenly it was time to leave. The house would be cared for by Sally and Jimson in their absence. Honor had a final glimpse of the mansion as they stowed themselves in the big touring car Mr. Stone had purchased especially for the trip. A strange desire to flee back to the security of the walls that had housed her for so many weeks and months touched Honor briefly and was gone. Ahead lay — what? Why should she suddenly long for her own room?

It was a long trip. By the time they arrived Laurene was tired, and she ordered Honor to see that Heather had a snack and was put to bed. Honor's heart beat quickly as she obeyed, anxious for her first sight of the canyon. She had already thrilled to the massiveness of El Tovar Hotel, built just after the turn of the century. Its native boulders and pine logs were different from anything she could have imagined, yet perfect for the setting. Grateful she could be alone for that all-important first sight of the canyon, she reassured Heather, promising she would get to do all the wonderful things the canyon offered while they were there.

Honor deliberately did not look into the canyon until she found a secluded spot a good distance away from the hotel. She kept her eyes fixed on a distant point of the far wall.

Her trembling fingers caught the twisted trunk of an old tree as she finally peered into a rent that could have been created only by the hand of God. She gazed down on mountaintops — and they were a mile high! No wonder writers described the canyon as indescribable. Nothing on earth could have prepared her for it. It was beautiful, awful, magnificent, terrible.

How long she stood gripping the tree she never knew. She turned away, only to look back at once. Every movement of light and shadow changed the canyon from red to purple, light to dark. It was impossible to grasp with the human mind — a never-ending, shifting panorama.

Honor tottered back, sinking down on the needle-covered ground. The sorrow of the

21

past months had been drawn from her by the sheer force of what lay before her. She shuddered. God had created all this and still sent His Son to die to save sinners — the God Granny said was waiting for her to accept Him. She tried to laugh and failed miserably. She deliberately brought up her losses: parents, Granny, Keith, home. No. Even such a God could not find place in her life after taking away everything precious. She could stand no more.

Yet after a simple dinner with Heather she again slipped into the evening's dimness. She watched until no light was left to reveal the canyon's secrets, an uneasy peace fighting with something inside clamoring for recognition. What if God really was calling her to accept His Son? Granny had talked time and again of those who were "under conviction" for their sins. Was this what she had meant, this terrible tearing apart inside? Part of her longed to fling herself to the ground and cry for mercy, while her head told her it was insane. More than likely it was just the effect of her illness and shock coupled with the beauty of this place.

Without warning a handsome face laughed in the still night air before her, leaving her drained. "I need someone," she whispered.

She laughed bitterly. First God — then a wraith from the past. If this was what happened when she came to Arizona, she'd better run back to San Francisco and find another job. Still the new idea tormented her. She needed someone to love and honor, to cherish, to fill her life. Overhead the bright Arizona stars seemed close enough to pick.

She had attended many weddings, seeing inner-most feelings and glimpsing what love between man and woman could be. She could even remember how her parents had been. It kept her from being attracted to a cheaper form of excitement. She would not accept second best. *Someday he will come,* she thought.

She caught her breath. Was this the recognition for which she had been brought to Arizona? In her soul, the searing certainty it was not shook her. What of the far greater truth she had so steadfastly denied?

Refusing to answer, she hurried toward the main entrance of El Tovar and dashed across the lobby. She heard a group clattering down the stairs before she saw them. The next instant she lay sprawled on the floor.

Honor looked up into the devastatingly handsome face of a dark-haired, dark-eyed man, who was apologizing and helping her up.

"I say! I've knocked you down with my clumsiness. I should have been watching where I was going."

His face changed. Delight, incredulity, and recognition mingled in rapid succession. "Honor? Honor Brooks?"

From her unladylike position Honor saw what her mind could not accept — the man who had knocked her flat was her soldier from long ago — Phillip Travis.

Phillip! He had come into her life like a whirlwind, appearing with a small group of soldiers who came to church one night. He had made a special point to talk with her afterward.

It was the beginning of a tremulous, butterfly world. Phillip's home was *Casa del Sol*, "House of the Sun," near Flagstaff, Arizona. Dark and handsome, he fit the storybook image of the knight in shining armor who would one day sweep her off her feet and carry her to his ranch to live happily ever after.

Honor's mouth twisted in a slight twinge of the pain she had suffered when he went overseas, promising to write and disappearing as suddenly as he had come. She wondered if he, too, had fallen in France. It

24

seemed inconceivable he would not have written, if he were able, after spending every free moment with her and Granny.

She could still remember his farewell. "Honor, I don't know if I'll be back. But would you wait for me? When I come home, will you marry me?"

Alarm had brushed gentle wings against her spirit and reason. "We hardly know each other!"

His gaze was compelling. Taking both her hands in his, he drew her unwillingly toward him, overriding the strange combination of longing and reluctance she felt.

"You can't tell me you don't care."

Honor had tried, but there was a biding-my-time look in his smile. "We will have time when I come home."

She had felt her heart pound as he promised, "I'll write."

2

Phillip drew her to her feet. "I'm sorry. I'm terribly sorry. You aren't hurt, are you?" He held her off with both hands, still clutching her wrists as she mutely shook her head. "Come in for dinner with us. We just arrived, and the dining room is still open."

Some of Honor's composure returned. "I have already eaten, Mr. Travis. Besides" — she glanced down at her white shirtwaist and plain dark skirt — "I'm not dressed for dinner."

"You look fine." He turned to a girl in the party. "Babs, tell Honor — Miss Brooks — she looks fine."

He didn't seem to catch the scowl on the pretty redhead's face as her social breeding forced her to respond. "Of course. Do come in for a cup of coffee, at least."

Phillip led her to a table. "Everyone, this is Honor Brooks." His ardent gaze made her uncomfortable. "She is the girl I told you all about, the one from San Francisco. Or did I? Anyway, now that I've found her again, I won't let her get away so easily!"

In spite of herself, Honor blushed. He made it sound as if she had once escaped

26

him when the opposite had been true. He was the one who had promised to write and never followed through.

The blush didn't escape Phillip. "A girl who blushes in this day and age? Will wonders never cease!" He waved a lazy arm toward his friends. "Mark, Cecile, Jon, Patti; you've already met Babs." There was something in his voice demanding recognition, but Honor had never heard of them before.

Phillip surveyed her with keen eyes. "When did you come? You've never been here before, have you?"

Honor was aware of her position in the split second before answering. She was also aware of how painfully crumpled her shirtwaist must be and how her hair was falling all over the place. "I'm here with Mr. and Mrs. Stone. He is an attorney in San Francisco."

Phillip's eyes widened in admiration. "I'd say he is! Everyone has heard of Ben Stone. I didn't know you knew him."

"I am his daughter's governess." Honor didn't miss the glance of scorn from Babs. Her chin came up. "After Granny died and when Keith didn't come home from France —" Suddenly the cloud of smoke around the table got to her. What was she doing here with this group of people? She had no part in their way of life. Phillip was the only one not smoking. Drinks were being poured.

She stumbled to her feet, throat thick from emotion and smoke. "Thank you for the coffee. I'll excuse myself now."

"Oh, I say, Miss Brooks!" Phillip trailed her to the door. "I'm sorry — about your grandmother and Keith, that is. I didn't know."

His sympathy was so sincere that she found herself smiling up at him through the gathering mist. "Thank you, and good night."

"You aren't going to run off from me, are you?" he demanded. "Not just when we've found each other again?"

Honor's heart leaped in spite of herself. The memory of his charm hadn't done him justice. Phillip Travis held an appeal for her that couldn't be denied. But what was he doing in such a crowd? Evidently he knew them well; they were his friends. He hadn't been like that in San Francisco. There had been no mention of smoking or drinking. He had called at her home and taken her to church. Sometimes they had taken long walks. Had he changed so much, or had she been wrong about him?

Phillip totally misunderstood her silence. "It isn't because you're working, is it?" He grinned. "I always thought I'd try it. They tell me it's fascinating." A hoot of derision came from the table they had just left, and Honor's face flamed. This was no place for her. Evidently Phillip was a member of the "pleasure seekers" or "parasites" as Mr. Stone classified such people.

"Thank you again for the coffee." Before Phillip could detain her she slipped away, but not before overhearing Babs cattily remark, "That girl walks like royalty."

Honor couldn't help smiling grimly to herself. Why not? Her family might not have been rich, but they were honorable. Why shouldn't she walk proudly?

Yet as she prepared for bed with a last glance out the window toward the canyon, her heart beat faster. Phillip was so handsome. There had been gentleness in his touch and voice as he spoke of Granny and Keith. For a moment it overruled the indolent arrogance she had sensed in him, an arrogance that was not in keeping with the long-held image in her heart. Did he still own the ranch, Casa del Sol? Her face cleared a bit. That might explain it. Perhaps he was an important man here in northern Arizona.

She remembered stumbling home, anxious to tell Granny about Phillip's proposal. She could still see the troubled look in the blue eyes, the lined face surrounded by curly white hair.

"Is he a Christian, Honor?"

"Who cares? I'm not, either."

Granny's gnarled hands lay still in her aproned lap. "I pray every day you will be."

Remorse filled her, mingled with anger. "I thought you liked Phillip!"

"He is courteous, charming, and utterly godless."

"That's not fair!" Honor's white face had waved battle flags of color. "After all, I met him in church."

Granny suddenly looked old. "Anyone can go to church, Honor. If he hasn't trusted the Lord Jesus Christ in his heart, his going to church doesn't mean anything." Granny's next words rang like a prophecy. "I believe someday you will accept our Lord, who has waited for you so long. I don't know what it's going to take to make you see you can't outrun God. When you do, if you are married to an unbeliever, your life will be misery." She softly quoted, " 'Be ye not unequally yoked together with unbelievers: for —' "

" '— for what fellowship hath righteousness with unrighteousness? and what communion hath light with darkness?' " Honor finished bitterly, noting the surprise in Granny's eyes. "Oh, yes, Granny, I know Second Corinthians six fourteen — you've made sure I know Scripture well. Too bad it just 'didn't take.' " She ignored the pain in Granny's face. "I'm going to wait for Phillip Travis. Besides, if God does catch up with me, there's no reason He can't catch Phillip, too."

In the following weeks, when no letter had come, Granny never mentioned Phillip. Neither did Honor. A new fear had touched her. If Phillip were dead she would never know. Should she write Casa del Sol? No. Phillip had not gone home before being shipped overseas. They wouldn't know she existed. Phillip had said he had one brother and seemed disinclined to say more, so she hadn't questioned him.

So long ago! Almost another lifetime. In the years since she first met Phillip she had been too busy and harried to meet other eligible men. Since coming to the Stones she had never gone to church. Granny was gone. She would not be a hypocrite. It couldn't be that her half-promise to wait for Phillip had haunted her, could it?

In weakness of spirit, Honor faced it

squarely. Ridiculous as it might seem, she had been bound to Phillip Travis. Until she knew for sure he was dead, she had not been able to accept another in his place.

Finally the excitement of the trip and the fresh air did its work. Honor could stay awake no longer.

She was awakened by a broad ray of sunlight crossing her room and Heather standing by her bedside.

"Miss Honor, just see!"

Heather's face was barely visible above the largest bouquet of flowers she had ever seen, eyes sparkling as Honor protested, "There must be a mistake! No one would be sending me flowers."

"It says H-O-N-O-R," Heather pointed out proudly, glad to show off her newly gained ability to recognize letters.

Honor took the flowers from her small charge and put them on the table. American Beauty roses, a wealth of them, catching the sunlight into their depths, filled the room with fragrance.

"Great Scot!" Laurene Stone had wandered into Honor's room. "Where did those come from?" She looked at Honor suspiciously.

"I don't know." Honor's clear gaze met Mrs. Stone's. "Oh, here's a card."

HAVE BREAKFAST WITH
ME, OR I WILL THINK
YOU HAVEN'T FORGIVEN
ME FOR RUNNING YOU
DOWN. I'LL BE IN THE
LOBBY WHENEVER
YOU'RE READY.

Phillip

Honor could feel her face heating as she silently passed the note to Mrs. Stone.

"Who is this Phillip?"

"Phillip Travis. He knocked me down when I was coming upstairs last night. I met him a few years ago when he was stationed in San Francisco."

"Phillip Travis! Not the one who owns that fabulous ranch here in Arizona — some Spanish name meaning sun?" New respect shone in Mrs. Stone's face. "How did you ever meet *him?*"

"He came to church with a group of soldiers. I suppose they were lonely for home." A reminiscent smile curved Honor's finely carved lips.

"Well, what are you waiting for? Get ready and meet him for breakfast."

Honor's memories faded. "I can't do that! He's here with a group. Besides" — she smiled at Heather — "we have all kinds of things to do today."

"He can join us for breakfast. I'm sure Ben will enjoy meeting him. Get Heather ready, and we'll meet downstairs as soon as possible." Mrs. Stone ended the discussion by sweeping out the door.

Honor stared open-mouthed after her employer's wife. Well! It certainly made a difference whom she knew. Mischief briefly touched her face, but she busied herself arraying Heather in a charming red dress, then quickly got ready herself. She hesitated, trying to decide what to wear, then firmly pushed aside the party dresses and settled for another shirtwaist, sparkling white and crisp. Her brown hair had been brushed and shone by the time she and Heather descended the stairs.

The Stones were already there, seated in a sunny corner. So was Phillip. Honor couldn't help the soft color that mounted to her hairline as she joined them.

Laurene Stone showed no traces of ill health this morning. "Honor, as you can see we went ahead and introduced ourselves. It's so important making good contacts right away when one goes into a strange land."

Honor disciplined a laugh at Mrs. Stone's implications. She didn't dare look at Phillip.

But a few minutes later she raised her head. "Thank you for the roses, Mr. Travis." In the time since she had learned Phillip really was an important person, she had also decided it had better be "Mr. Travis." She had no right to presume on former friendship.

Phillip would have none of it. "Make it Phillip, all of you." His glance included the Stones but returned to Honor. "Perhaps I'd better introduce myself a little more, Mrs. Stone. My brother and I own a cattle ranch just north of Flagstaff. He actually does most of the work, but I —"

"A real ranch? With cowboys?" Heather broke her usual silence around strangers, with a frankly hero-worshiping look.

"Real cowboys." His smile at the little girl was endearing. The next moment he leaned toward her. "Miss Heather, how would you like to visit that ranch when you leave here?"

"Oh, Daddy, Mother, could we?"

"Really, Mr. Travis — Phillip." Ben Stone's face was dart with annoyance. "We have barely met. Heather shouldn't have hinted."

"I didn't hint, Daddy. He 'vited us." Heather's lip trembled, and her clear eyes filled with tears.

"That's right." Phillip had never been more charming. "I really mean it. Casa del

35

Sol is a sprawling hacienda with room for a dozen people. We love company. Our housekeeper, Mama Rosa, likes nothing better than cooking for a housefull."

Honor was amazed at how quickly Mr. Stone capitulated. "If it isn't an imposition. I really have always wanted to visit a working cattle ranch." He grinned. "My doctor told us to get out of doors. I'm sure he'd approve!"

"Then it's settled. Whenever you're ready to leave the canyon, let me know. I'll go on ahead and get ready for you." He turned back to Heather. "We even have ponies just your size."

She smiled delightedly as he added, "Oh, by the way, you must take the mule trip into the canyon while you're here."

"Not I!" Laurene Stone threw her hands up in mock horror. "I'm going to spend my time right here in this lodge. Some of our San Francisco friends are coming, and we already have bridge games arranged. The rest of you can take care of the outdoor life." She lifted one shoulder daintily. "I'm sure my husband and Honor will want to go. I can keep Heather with me."

"Oh, Mama!" Heather's face fell with disappointment. "Can't I ride a mule?"

Again Honor was impressed by Phillip

Travis's quick evaluation of the situation. He leaned across to Heather once more. "Those mules are pretty big, Heather. How about riding down the trail with me? I've been several times, and it's always a little lonely on the mule's back. You can fit in the saddle just in front of me."

Mr. Stone looked worried. "Are these donkeys safe?"

"Not donkeys, sir. Mules. Our donkeys are smaller and known as burros, or 'Arizona Nightingales.' " Phillip laughed. "You won't believe it when you hear them bray. The mules that go down in the canyon are trained beyond belief. The trainers flap slickers at them, do everything in the world to startle them before they are even allowed on the trail.

"You know, the little burros have been given a rather unique legend." An unusual softness crept into his voice. "It is said Jesus put a cross on the back of each burro as a reward for service. The old prospectors believe it. If you look at a burro's shoulders, you'll see that cross. Some are plainer than others, but there is a more or less distinct marking on every burro's back."

He paused, smiling again. "Our burros have saved countless lives. They are not only good pets but the prospector's best friend. They are also sturdy. Now *mules* are different — ornery. Wait until you get on a trail edge and your mule decides to reach over the side to chomp grass. I do believe the good Lord created them with a sense of humor!"

Honor's eyes sparkled. Had she been wrong about Phillip and his friends? He spoke so easily of the legend and the good Lord's creation. He was quite a man. The man for her? The thought was enough to fill her face with a shine and set her heart pounding.

The rest of the meal passed swiftly. Heather's laughter rang out at the witty remarks of Phillip, who seemed to take delight in talking with her. When they finished he said, "I don't want to intrude, but since I do know the canyon, would you consider taking me on as a guide?"

Even Honor was touched by the wistfulness in his question, and the keen glance of Mr. Stone seemed to be weighing Phillip's sincerity.

"I really mean it. My crowd has been here so often the thrill is gone. It will be like seeing it for the first time, showing you everything there is to see."

"We would be happy to have you with us for whatever time you have free," Mr. Stone told him.

"Then I'll be with you all the time!" His dark eyes twinkled. "Just wait and see!"

Phillip became the perfect host. First he introduced Laurene to several avid card players he knew. By the time her San Francisco friends arrived, she was already part of a well-established circle that widened to include them. Her reaction to the Grand Canyon had been a shiver and, "What a terrible hole in the ground!" Then she settled into a daily routine of sleeping late, breakfasting in bed, and meeting with friends for cards, followed by a leisurely preparation and donning of exquisite gowns for dinner each night.

Ben Stone lost his paleness in the hours he spent outdoors. Sometimes with just Heather, more often as part of the foursome with Honor and Phillip, he radiated happiness. Once when Honor found him alone on the canyon rim as sunset threw mocking banners into the sky to reflect on the panorama before them, she tried to thank him.

"I am the one in debt, Honor." He waved into the ever-changing shadows of night creeping toward the canyon. "I didn't realize how I needed to get away — until I used you as an excuse to come!" A look of reverence shown through his level gaze. "No one could look on such a scene and not believe in a Creator, could they?"

"No, Mr. Stone." But he had already turned back to the canyon, now murky in is depths, leaving Honor feeling she had been forgotten.

Honor was free for a time each afternoon when Heather took a nap and after she had gone to bed. Phillip gradually filled those moments until it became a usual thing for him to be waiting when she came down. Several days after they arrived he asked her if she would walk with him. Something in his look stirred her. The afternoon was bright. Birds called, and squirrels ran along the canyon edge, looking for bits of dropped food.

Honor's hand trembled as she dressed carefully and brushed her bright hair into waves. Was the pale blue dress too fussy? When she had told Phillip the clothes were "made over," he had covered his surprise by commenting how clever she was with a needle.

As they skirted the outcroppings of rock to find a quiet place in full view of the canyon but not the hotel, Honor noted how quiet Phillip had grown. Was there some significance in this particular invitation?

"Honor, will you be my girl?"

She was speechless.

"I mean it." He doggedly forced her to look at him, compelling with his eyes. "You know I was in love with you in San Francisco. I even asked you if you would wait for me. Don't you remember?"

She could only remain silent, unspoken words dying on her lips.

"I know I treated you shabbily, going off and not writing after I promised. But Honor, I've had a lot of time since then to consider." He looked deep into her eyes. "I love you, Honor." Without asking permission he caught her close and tried to kiss her.

She sprang back. "Why did you do that? Why did you have to spoil everything?" Vexation steadied her trembling lips. "We barely know each other!"

"Don't you believe in love at first sight?"

She wanted to shout no, but couldn't do it. She remembered the feeling she had had when they first met, the same feeling that had intensified beyond belief since meeting him again at the canyon. "How can I take you seriously? You don't even know me, not really."

"I know you well enough to know I'm going to get ahead of Mark and Jon." His jaw set stubbornly. "I saw how they watched you, even the night you came. I'm

41

putting my bid in first."

"I'm not up for grabs, you know."

His mouth twisted in an odd smile. "You think I don't know that? I'm twenty-nine years old, Honor Brooks. I've known a lot of women. You think I can't tell the difference between real and imitation? You're what my grandmother calls 'a real lady.' There aren't many of them around these days." He pushed back a lock of hair. "I don't want second best."

From the corridors of memory came Honor's own words, *I'll never settle for second best.* It brought hot blood to her face. "I'm sorry, Phillip. You have your friends. I'm here working, a vacation job. I'm not looking for summer romance."

"And you think I am?" A surge of color filled his own face. He gritted his teeth, obviously trying to control anger as he gazed across the canyon, seeming to find in its depths strength to calm himself. "What right have you to judge me? I've waited all my life for a girl like you — and that's what you are, a girl, in spite of being almost twenty-four, as you told me. I'll wager you haven't lived those twenty-four years without getting some knowledge of human nature. I fell for you when I first met you. Then with the war and all, you slipped back in memory." His voice deepened. "Then I came here — and found you. When I picked you up from the floor I fell for you — hard. I'd begun to think I'd never find the girl I wanted to marry. Sure, I've had all kinds of girls and women, even considered marrying a few of them, but never did. Men have ideal women, too, you know." The mobile mouth curved in a smile. "If you can honestly tell me you felt nothing when I picked you up, I'll apologize and get lost."

Honor couldn't speak. Only the strength of his hold kept her from falling. When he had spoken of wondering if the "right" person would ever appear, she had identified with him in a quick rush of sympathy. Was her heart trying to tell her something? Was she stubbornly refusing to listen? Had Phillip really been searching — for her?

"You can't do it, can you? Then think about this." Gently he drew her to him, kissing her on the lips. Startled, she broke from him like a shy fawn and fled back the way they had come, only to be followed by his exultant cry, "I'm going to marry you, Miss Honor Brooks — and you're going to like it!"

When she reached her room she was breathless. Tears stood in her eyes, brilliant, refusing to fall. Futilely she bathed her hot face, demanding of her image, "How did he dare?" Yet the gentle touch of his kiss stayed on her lips even after she had furiously scrubbed them. The walls of the room she had found so charming now closed in on her. She must get free. She caught up her sweater and slipped out, carefully checking the lobby to make sure she was unseen. In her walks between El Tovar and the canyon rim, Honor had noticed a secluded spot. She headed for it. Would the canyon reach out to her, slow her whirling emotions?

"What if he meant it?" Honor gazed into the chasm, unaware of anything except the lingering pressure of Phillip's lips on her own. "I love him!"

A cloud flitted across the sun, sending a curious mist to the canyon. To Honor's excited fancy Granny's face seemed to float there with accusing eyes. Her wanting about marrying any unbeliever rang in Honor's heart. With it came the memory of Phillip as he had been that first night in the dining room — surrounded by smoke and the tangy odor of liquor. Her heart quailed. In spite of not acknowledging Christ as Lord, Honor abhorred cheapness, and to her smoking and drinking fell in that category.

"But Phillip was not smoking or drinking," she protested brokenly. The mist disappeared, and her rebellion burst its bonds. All Honor's accumulated misery during the hard years gathered in one great force, just as the massive clouds overhead mustered forces to batter the earth. She sprang to her feet. "I will not give him up! I know now I loved Phillip even when he told me good-bye. It's been there all the time. That's why I have felt bound."

A crack of lightning followed by a burst of cannonlike thunder halted the words, striking fear into her heart. She would not bow before it. "Where were You when I gave You a chance, God? Where was the love You told of in those verses I learned when I promised to try and know You better if you'd spare Keith? Or when I begged for a job and only got one by chance? Everything I've ever loved has been taken away. I will not give up Phillip!"

She raised her face in defiance, as if to challenge the very storm itself. It had increased in intensity, pelting the earth with raindrops the size of hailstones, kicking up dust and turning it to red mud. "If Granny was right, if misery is ahead —" she caught her breath at the possibility and again hardened her voice "— I'll pay the price for the happiness I'll have in between."

She sank to the ground, not heeding the

violent storm soaking her, turning her into a muddy, crumpled figure. For better or worse, she had chosen. Why should another verse learned years before haunt her at this moment? It was Joshua 24:15 — *"Choose you this day whom ye will serve . . . but as for me and my house, we will serve the LORD."* She impatiently refused to admit her slight hesitation, replacing it with Phillip's laughing face. He would ask her again to marry him. Next time there would be no hesitation. After all, hadn't he said he'd known all kinds of girls and women?

Some of her triumph faded. Had he kissed those others the way he did her? She would never tell him he was the only one who had kissed her, but she was glad. She had kept her promise and waited; he had come differently than expected. With a smile, she returned to the present. If she had wanted solitude at the canyon, she had it. No one would be out in this storm.

But she had been wrong. A dark shape hurried toward her. "Honor! I've looked everywhere for you." His voice was filled with fear, for her, she knew. Suddenly all her troubles were gone. Phillip had come for her.

"I'm here, Phillip. You've found me."

He peered into her face, seeing the way it

46

was turned to him.

"Honor!" The next moment she was caught close in an embrace that deepened as she sighed and relaxed against him. Surely it must be right when she felt so happy. She lifted her mouth, and in the storm on the canyon's edge, returned Phillip's kiss. She didn't care if the storm never let up. She had fought so long against the fact of her family's death, it was sheer heaven to lean on someone stronger.

This time it was Phillip who broke away. "Honor — you care. To kiss me like that — a girl like you — it must mean you care." He caught her in his arms, carrying her slight frame, running back through the rain as if he would never let her go.

"Put me down, Phillip! What will they all say?" She struggled furiously, but he rained more kisses on her wet mouth and hair.

"Who cares? We'll announce our engagement at dinner tonight." He set her down just inside the door, still with his arms around her, his face lit up with triumph.

"Engagement!" A cold chill went through her. "Phillip, you're mad. We can't announce an engagement now."

Doubt crept into his face, and his reply was cynical. "Then you're like the rest of them? Lead a man on and toss him aside?"

It hit her cruelly. "Phillip! Of course I'm not like that. It's just too soon — no one would ever understand. I'm not sure I understand myself." She blushed. "What would the Stones think?"

His face softened, and he took both her hands in his. "It's all right, Honor. I'm sorry." One lock of wet hair dangled in front of his eyes, making him look like a truant schoolboy. "You're absolutely right. We'll wait and announce it at the end of your vacation here."

"We'll see." She knew her color heightened under his ardent gaze. "Now if you don't mind, I'd like to get into some other clothes."

Phillip threw back his head and laughed. "You look like a drowned squirrel. Run along, my dear, and meet me back down here when you've changed."

The glow and tingle of Honor's skin wasn't all caused by her stinging shower. Phillip loved her. Phillip Travis loved her! She raced through her dressing. She mustn't wait one minute longer than necessary. She wanted every bit of time with him she could find. To think, a few weeks ago she had been a poor, forsaken person feeling sorry for herself. Today she was loved — and loved in return. Memories of her parents' happy years glorified her feeling for Phillip.

"Tell me about your home," she urged as they sat together on a big couch in the lobby later. They had eluded his friends, who were going to a dance. Phillip had wickedly whispered, "I don't want any man's arms around you but mine." Honor's heart had pounded. Dancing was another thing she didn't do.

Now Phillip relaxed against the couch and stared into the huge fireplace with its dancing flames. "I suppose the story goes back to my great-grandfather. He married a wealthy Spanish girl, and they acquired Casa del Sol."

"House of the Sun," she translated.

"You know Spanish?" He sounded surprised.

"No, I — I remembered." She wouldn't tell him how she had treasured the phrase all the long, lonely months after he went away.

"Funny, I love it even though I'm not there much. Too busy having a good time. Now that you'll be there with me —" His look said volumes.

Honor hastily changed the subject. "Phillip, Babs looked at me tonight as if she hated me."

"Babs and I grew up together, had a lot of fun. I even would have married her a few years ago. She turned me down cold. Now if she wants me back it's just too bad."

She was shocked by his callousness but soothed as he added, "Babs and I are alike — too selfish, demanding. I won't be that way with you." There was an air of humility about him that Honor sensed was foreign to his nature.

"I'm glad you told me, Phillip. Now let's forget it. If she didn't care a few years ago, she probably doesn't care now." But when Honor entered her room that night, lips still tingling from Phillip's goodnight kiss, she gasped in dismay.

Seated in the chair by the window, Babs waited, enmity in every fold of her exquisite green gown.

"Do come in." Her voice was mocking. "It *is* your room."

"What are you doing here?" Honor barely had breath to ask. She had been shaken to turn from Phillip and suddenly meet the girl he had once loved.

"I thought we should perhaps have a little talk. You seem to be occupied during the day and evening, so I came here." She motioned insolently to the bed. "You might as well sit down, I intend to be here for some time."

Honor wondered if her shaking knees

would carry her that far. "If you are going to tell me all about you and Phillip, you don't need to bother. I already know. He told me."

"Did he indeed! I doubt that he told you *all* about us." The green eyes glittered like algae in a lake, murky and treacherous. "Did he tell you that we have been engaged for years?" She held out a long white hand with blood-red nails. A huge emerald winked a wicked eye from the third finger.

3

Honor felt as if she had been stabbed. "Engaged?"

"Of course." Was pity mixed with anger in the other's eyes? "Don't be a little fool. Every time we go on a jaunt Phillip finds a girl. Not always one like you, I'll have to admit. But when vacation's over, he forgets. Didn't he do just that when he left you in San Francisco?" She hardened again. "He knows we will marry when I get ready. Maybe even soon."

"I don't believe you." The sinking feeling in Honor's heart belied her words.

"I suggest you think about it. Don't rush into anything. Once Phillip gets away from the canyon and you, well, he will laugh at his romantic little interlude." Babs rose, magnificently stretching to full height like a sleek cat. "Let him go. It's for your own good."

Strength born of fear flowed through Honor, as she remembered little things about Phillip. She must defend herself — and him. "Phillip will be going first. He has asked the Stones and me to visit Casa del Sol. Even if they have to leave, Phillip says

Mama Rosa will chaperone me."

"You can bet your sweet life on that!"

Honor ignored the bitter interruption. "We won't get married until we have time to know each other. When we do, I'll be Mrs. Phillip Travis, and nothing can change it!"

"I wouldn't count on it." Babs glided toward the door. "I wonder what Phillip's brother will say about you." Her laugh brought color to Honor's face. "He's a hundred years older than Phillip in outlook."

"That's why Phillip is going first." Honor wished she had bitten her tongue when she saw the triumph on Babs's face. "Phillip is sincere —"

"I thought so." The redhead pounced on the first half of Honor's statement. "As far as sincere — Phillip wouldn't recognize the meaning of the word if it bit him on his handsome nose. If you expect sincerity, you'd better run as far and fast as you can from Phillip Travis." Babs's eyes shifted, then fixed their cold stare on Honor. "You're one of those do-gooders, aren't you? Then don't deliberately walk into a lion's den." She must have caught Honor's look of surprise. "I went to church — a long time ago, before I met Phillip. Don't think you can change him."

Honor felt herself stiffen. "I'm sure your

advice is well-meant, but I believe I know what the real Phillip Travis is like. I am going to marry him someday."

Honor could see emotions warring in Babs's face — pity, disgust, hatred, contempt. Pity won. "Then, my dear little governess, may the gods have mercy on you. You'll need it."

The door opened and closed behind her, leaving Honor alone — more alone than she had been even waiting for Keith to come home. The storm in the canyon was as nothing compared to the storm in her heart. Incredible as it seemed, Babs did love Phillip. Then why hadn't she married him when she had the chance? Honor shivered, remembering the callous way Phillip had spoken of Babs. What if he were to say the same about her? No! Her shocked, white face in the mirror denied the traitorous thought. Phillip loved her. Yet hadn't he loved Babs when he once asked her to marry him?

Minutes ticked into hours, and the questions did not cease. Once Honor thought of digging out the Bible Granny had given her so long ago, but discarded the idea. She had made her choice, forfeited her right to expect God's help. She might not be a Christian, but she did know Scripture, and

God didn't bless those who deliberately turned away from Him. With the first touch of dawn she slipped to the stairs. She would get away from her accusing walls.

As she descended the stairs she heard the clink of silver and laughter from those who were preparing the dining room for breakfast. For a moment she envied the happy workers who came from all over the United States to work with the summer crowds at the canyon. The next moment she slipped outside and ran to the canyon's edge.

"It's unbelievable!" A small squirrel eyed her in alarm and scuttled away. Honor's eyes were no longer heavy. The early morning canyon mists had driven away need for sleep.

How could it be so different, bathed in the almost-ethereal glow of morning? She had seen it in daylight, darkness, storm. Now it had changed completely. No wonder she had read that she wouldn't see the canyon, but experience it.

Honor pulled her cape closer against the chill morning air, watching lazy patches of mist yield to the insistent sun. A tug within reminded her of the struggle from the night before. Some of the beauty dimmed. Why couldn't she put aside the childhood teachings now she had made her choice? Must they forever haunt her?

The sun burst over the canyon wall after sending heralding streaks to announce its arrival. "If only Keith were here!" she cried to the warming rays. But Keith wasn't here. He would never see the canyon. Her face hardened. If he had come back, perhaps she could have accepted the Lord he believed in so strongly. But not now. She had her life to live, and the splendor around her showed that the world could still be beautiful. She would find strength for whatever might come, but not through Christ.

"Good morning, my darling."

Honor whirled from the canyon, feeling betraying color flooding her face. Phillip was standing a few feet away. His appearance shocked her. Where was the frightening man Babs had described? This was Phillip, eyes soft, hand outstretched — the same Phillip who had come for her in the storm the day before.

"I thought I would find you here." He led her a little apart from the other sightseers, seeking privacy beneath the spreading branches of a tall, gnarled tree. "You're even more beautiful in the morning sunlight than you are drenched from a storm!"

Relief filled Honor until she would have fallen if he had not held her arm. Still she could not speak. It was the same as coming from the storm into a lighted room — protected, safe, secure. She raised her face to his.

"You're the sweetest girl on earth, Honor." His husky whisper brought her back.

"And you're the most wonderful man." She was rewarded by a look of almost-humility in his face.

"I don't deserve you, you know."

Honor felt a strange surge of power and covered it by agreeing. "Of course not!"

Phillip's expression changed to match her gaiety. "You rascal! Let's get some breakfast. We're signed up for the mule trip into the canyon, and it will be leaving soon."

"We are what?" Honor's eyes filled with horror. "You won't get me on any mule going down there!" Her scornful finger indicated a narrow, winding path leading down along the gigantic rock walls, melting into infinity around a bend.

"Of course I will. Ben and Heather can hardly wait to get started. I thought you were excited about going."

"I was," she confessed in a small voice, "until I saw the trail."

"You'll be fine." Phillip innocently added, "Even Babs went last year, and you know she isn't about to go in any danger."

She eyed him suspiciously, then relaxed. "If I fall in the canyon it will be on your conscience."

"You don't really think I'd ever take you where it was unsafe, do you?" Phillip's gaze settled her more than anything else could have done. "You'll be as safe as home in your rocking chair. Ben will be right behind you; Heather and I will be in front of you."

But when breakfast was over and they were ready to go she couldn't help trying once more, appealing to Phillip when the others weren't listening. "Are you sure you want me to go? What if I faint?" She didn't tell him she had never fainted in her entire life. "I'd slow down the whole group."

"Look at me!" Heather piped up, already seated on the mule Phillip would ride. She looked so tiny Honor had another qualm. "She'll be all right, won't she?"

"With me here?" Phillip just smiled. "Simple as riding a rocker." He helped her mount a shaggy beast who turned and looked her over, then disinterestedly went back to cropping the sparse grass by the trail. She found herself patting his shoulders timidly, wishing he were a little burro with a cross, instead of just an ornery mule.

"We won't stay overnight this time,"

Phillip told her. "Next time, after we're married —"

"Next time!" Honor glared. "If you think there will be a —"

"As I was saying." He flashed his famous grin. "They are talking of building a real accommodation in the bottom of the canyon. Phantom Ranch, I think it will be called. But this time we'll just stop for lunch, then climb back out this afternoon. We go down several thousand feet. It will be hot." He looked approvingly at her lightweight jacket, which could be removed. "It's going to be a real pleasure educating you in all the things you've never done before, Honor."

Honor's face flamed. Would she always blindly follow his lead, trailing along as she was now trailing on her mule? Her natural common sense and good humor took over.

So what if she did? She'd lead him, too — but in more subtle ways. She clutched her reins, eyes sparkling, and looked straight ahead.

"Don't look down," the guide warned as they rounded a hairpin curve what seemed like eons later. Honor had slid off her jacket, and the warm sun hit her back with its rays.

"Close your eyes if you like, and don't be scared," Phillip called.

What now? Honor had swallowed her

heart countless times already. One by one the mules ahead slowed, then doubled back on themselves to disappear around the hairpin bend. Closer and closer Honor came until she reached the edge of eternity. Her eyes were fixed straight ahead as she had been told — until Old Baldy's neck shot downward, over the edge of the rim. Involuntarily Honor glanced down, following the line of ears with her gaze, and froze. It was terrible. It was grand. It was the worst thing that had ever happened to her.

"You're doin' fine, miss." The guide's brown face split into a white smile. "Forgot to tell you. Old Baldy always likes to chop a little grass right here." He didn't seem to notice how the reins were being held in a death grip that whitened her knuckles. "Just let him eat a bit and he'll make the turn just fine."

Honor couldn't have answered if her life had depended on it — and maybe it did. She just sat. Old Baldy finished his leisurely munching, turned, and followed the others. The weakness seeping through her almost unseated Honor, but with trembling fingers she managed to clutch the reins and smile weakly. She had kept herself from screaming. Now she even managed to smile at Heather.

From that point on, nothing frightened Honor. She had faced the worst with silence. Even the splash of Old Baldy's hooves as he forged through a creek at the bottom of the canyon didn't daunt her. When she fell off her mule into Phillip's arms, it was triumphantly. He need never know the last mile of trail had been managed by sheer determination.

"Well, Honor, wasn't it worth it?"

She gazed around her, really seeing the canyon bottom for the first time. The valley floor lay before her, an oasis of lush greenness. The burbling Colorado River ran red and sluggish. She was glad she had not had to cross that!

"It's —" She couldn't find words.

Phillip tenderly smoothed back clinging tendrils of damp hair from her hot face. "I know. That's why I come here."

Again she was aware of depths within him that did not ordinarily show. Her heart gave a great leap of joy. Surely he would understand and accept the way of life she had chosen, once they were married and she was able to tell him the happiness she had found in it.

"I feel like a glutton," Honor confessed later as she surveyed the shambles of her plate. "I didn't realize anyone could be so hungry!"

"Remarkable how fresh air and exercise can work up an appetite, isn't it?" The grizzled guide had seated himself next to Honor. "Nothing ever tastes so good as outdoor food. Say, if you're going to be around long, you should plan on some of the other canyon trips. You did a good job today. I'd say you could even tackle some of the rough trails."

"Rough trails! You mean this one isn't?" Honor was astonished.

"Of course not. This one's for beginners and tenderfeet." The guide turned away and didn't catch Honor's expression.

Phillip did, and laughed. "Don't look so shocked, Honor. This is Arizona."

All the way through the rest time and back up the canyon she thought of what Phillip had said. Arizona. It was everything she had dreamed of and more. Soft color stole to her hairline. "Phillip, when — when we're married, would you show me Arizona? All of it?"

"Fervently." The meaning in his one word sent a glow through her. What a change it was, being cared for and protected. The contrast between these past few days and her bleak life since the death of her parents brought a quick rush of emotion to Honor. How could she doubt Phillip in any way when he was so ready to please her?

By the time they got back it was growing a bit dusky. This time Honor didn't fall off Old Baldy, she had to be helped off. "What's wrong with my legs?"

"You're going to be pretty stiff young lady," the guide warned her. "Take a hot bath and get to bed early. You'll be hobbling a bit tomorrow."

The dire prediction came true. Not only was she hobbling, but Honor also found it took her three tries to get out of bed! Only Phillip's note telling her he'd wait and have breakfast when she did spurred her on.

"Miss Honor, are you going to marry Mr. Travis?" Heather's face was innocent in front of the huge bow in her blonde hair.

Before Honor could reply, Phillip said, "I certainly hope so."

"Well!" Mrs. Stone looked as if the breath had been knocked from her. "Why haven't you told us, Honor?"

Phillip came to her rescue, adroitly drawing attention away from the scarlet cheeks above her high-necked white shirt-waist. "She was afraid you'd think it a little sudden."

"Isn't it?"

Honor caught Ben Stone's frown and found her tongue. "I knew Phillip years ago

— he was in San Francisco —" She sounded incoherent even to herself. "I guess I never forgot him, and —"

Mrs. Stone cut her off by congratulating Phillip. But Mr. Stone whispered. "Are you happy, Honor?"

"Yes." Joy suffused her face with even more color. "He's everything I ever wanted." Was that a disappointed look in her employer's eyes? Honor pushed the thought aside. How could anyone be disappointed with Phillip?

There was something she must determine now the engagement had been announced. In their favorite spot by the canyon Honor watched Phillip teasing a frisky squirrel, wondering how to approach him.

"What are you thinking?" he demanded.

It was the perfect opening. "How glad I am I found you again."

A dark flush stained his face. "Was it you who found me? I thought I found you."

"What difference does it make?"

"None, to me." His arms reached for her, but she leaned back.

"Phillip do —" her voice trembled "— do you care dreadfully for drinking and all that?"

He sat up abruptly and stared at her. "What are you? A preacher?"

It was her turn to flush. "No. I just wondered." She took a deep breath. "I just don't believe in those things." Her voice was small. "I don't know how well I'll fit in your world — or you in mine."

"I'm a heathen, Honor." He didn't catch her involuntary look of dismay. A steel hand seemed to squeeze her heart. She had known he was no Christian and accepted it. But this —

"Do you believe in God?"

"Doesn't everyone?" He waved an indolent hand toward the canyon. "It took a Master Plan to build that."

Honor turned her head to hide her feelings, scarcely able to sort them out. Why did she feel disappointed at his statement? What did she have to lose when she had already put God aside?

"I don't care about drinking when I have you. You can do with me what you like. I'm weak with the crowd. You're seeing the best of me here."

In spite of the heat waves bouncing off the colorful canyon walls Honor felt a chill trickle down her spine. "You have everything, Phillip. Why follow the crowd?"

A somber shadow crossed his face. "Because of my brother. If he weren't so competent maybe I would be stronger. He thinks it's easier to do everything himself than wait for me to do it. He's right." The shadow deepened. "Don't get me wrong. I love him more than anyone on earth except you, but if he would shove me out and tell me to sink or swim I would be better off."

"What a terrible thing to say!"

"Is it?" Phillip's face contorted. "Let's forget it, kiddo. We'll be happy like they are." He pointed to a bird singing his heart out to his mate.

Honor's throat constricted as she matched the change of mood. Now was no time to preach. Deep inside resentment of the way Phillip's brother treated him began to grow. Was be an ogre? Even Babs had said he was a hundred years older in out-look. He must be an old fogey, set in his ways. She could just see him: burly; a little uncouth, perhaps, in spite of being the charming Phillip's brother.

Her lips set. She would not build up dis-like before meeting him. But once she was established at Casa del Sol she intended to have a little talk with Phillip's brother.

4

Incredible as it seemed, summer was nearly over. Mr. Stone reluctantly told them at breakfast one morning, "My business is piling up back home." He looked across at Phillip. "I don't want to rush you, but if you still want us to visit your ranch, it will have to be soon."

Phillip rose to the occasion gracefully. "Of course I do! I'll go ahead myself, maybe even leave today. We'll be waiting for you when you come." The look he gave Honor brought flags flying in her cheeks. That afternoon while Heather napped, Phillip led Honor to their private spot by the canyon's edge.

"It's only the beginning, you know." He looked deep into her eyes, and she bit back the impulse to deny it. Ever since she had known he was to leave and go ahead without her a strange — was it premonition? — had filled her. Perhaps it was because she had overheard Babs say, "About time we were leaving, old thing. It's getting a little tiresome here this time. I'll ride with you, of course."

Phillip evidently didn't sense how lost

Honor felt. He was going on about what a wonderful time they'd have at Casa del Sol and how she would love being mistress of the ranch.

"Phillip —" Must her voice shake? Something terrifying gripped her, as if she stood on a high pinnacle, ready to be swept away forever. "Do you really think I can make you happy?"

His eyes warmed. Taking both her hands in his own he drew her close, forcing her to look directly into his eyes. "I am the one who should be asking that." The humility so strange to his nature surfaced again. "You are everything I ever wanted, and much more than I deserve. Fate has been kind."

Honor's own eyes brimmed. If Phillip felt like that, helping him find happiness away from his wild companions should not be such a mountainous task.

Then he was gone. A final kiss, a careless wave, and Phillip Travis disappeared around the bend, leaving a strangely silent canyon.

At first Honor felt bereft. Then she sternly snapped out of it. She was here to be with Heather and was touched when Heather said, "I like Mr. Travis. He was a'f'ly nice about taking us places." She skipped alongside of Honor on the trail to

68

the rim, and her hand slid confidingly into Honor's. "But it's nice just us, isn't it? Like it was back home."

Compunction filled Honor. Had she neglected her duties to Heather because of Phillip? She silently shook her head. No, her times with Phillip alone had been while Heather slept or was otherwise occupied. She hugged the little girl hard, knowing how much she would miss her. "Yes, it is."

Heather stopped short under a huge pine, feet planted firmly in the needle-carpeted ground. "You won't be going home with us, will you? Mama says you'll stay at that ranch." Her bright little face clouded over. "What am I going to do without you?"

Honor had dreaded the moment but was prepared. "I talked with your mama and daddy. Heather, they've decided to let you go to school this fall. You'll be six, and it's time. You're going to have a wonderful time. You already know your letters so you'll be ahead of some of the others. There will be other boys and girls and —"

"You mean it?" The rainbow back of her tears chased smiles all over Heather's face. "Oh, Miss Honor, that's next best to having you!" She clapped her hands and bounced in glee. "But first we get to go to the ranch and ride ponies. Mr. Travis promised."

But Heather was doomed to disappointment.

Ben Stone's face was filled with distress as he came into the dining room, where the rest of their party waited for him so they could start dinner. "A case is coming up, and I must go back tomorrow. I didn't think it would be until later, but I must get home — right away."

"But the ranch," Heather wailed. "What about our visit — and Honor?"

Mr. Stone sighed. "Honor can go ahead with her plans. I believe it's only a matter of weeks until she is being married. I'll hire a car and driver to take her to Casa del Sol."

"But won't you need me on the way back to San Francisco?"

"My dear!" Ben Stone didn't catch his wife's look at the involuntary endearment. Neither did he see her eyes narrow, noticing how beautiful Honor had grown during her stay at the canyon. He was too intent on expressing gratitude. "We are in your debt. You will be well chaperoned by Mama Rosa. Perhaps we can visit another time."

Laurene's words fell like hard, cold rocks, every trace of former friendliness gone. "My husband," she emphasized the words, "is right. I am perfectly capable of handling Heather on the way home."

70

Honor was shocked at the fury in her face, then comprehension came. The woman was *jealous!* It was all Honor could do to quietly stand. "I'll start packing right away. I really am not hungry." She escaped with face burning, humiliated by the unjust accusation in Mrs. Stone's eyes.

Her last night at the canyon was filled with troubled dreams, darkness, hands reaching out. She awoke bathed in perspiration, calling out, "Phillip!" Was something wrong at the ranch? Could Phillip have been hurt? She had never given much heed to dreams, but this one left her unnerved.

The driver Mr. Stone hired was taciturn. While the tires nibbled away the miles Honor had time to reflect. Bitterness toward Mrs. Stone gradually was replaced by pity. What a terrible way to live, suspecting even a hired governess of trying to capture a loved one! She determinedly put the thoughts aside. It was a glorious time to be in Arizona. Already the leaves were beginning to show color. She could picture the bold and golden way the land would look later.

"Take the road toward Kendrick Peak," Phillip had instructed. "About five miles out there is a sign pointing north. Just stay on the road to Casa del Sol. We've had it graded."

His casual directions should have prepared her. They hadn't. She saw the turnoff, then the sign boldly blazoned over an arched entrance and cut into a wooden frame, almost as if in a trance. They drove down an endless, tree-lined lane. Honor marveled, even pinching herself to be sure it was real. It was.

Finally they swung around a gentle curve and stopped. The driver unloaded her bags, murmured a quick good-bye and was gone, leaving her staring ahead. Before her lay a mansion, reminiscent of old Spanish dons. Phillip had said it was a Spanish hacienda. He hadn't told her how the warm cream walls and the red tile roof nestled into the hills as if it had been created there. He hadn't told her that it was built around a courtyard. Through an open iron gate, she glimpsed a fountain, flowers, even singing birds. Weakly she leaned against the lacy iron work. It was too much. How could she ever belong to such a kingdom?

Memory of Babs's taunt flashed through her mind. Honor's chin came up. She would fit in. She would show them all. She and Phillip loved each other, and it was all that was important. It steadied her, but as she slowly approached the great carved door her heart fluttered. Would Phillip seem a

little unapproachable here in his own setting?

"May I help you?" Liquid brown eyes in a
round face above a spotless white apron
looked at her curiously as the door opened.

"Mama Rosa!" Honor impulsively held
out her hand, taking the older woman's
hand in her own.

"You know me?" The puzzle had not left
the housekeeper's face.

"Oh, yes. Phillip has told me all about
you."

"Oh. Felipe. You are his friend? Come in.
You are welcome."

"I am —" What check chained her tongue
from adding "his fiancee"? "I am his
friend," Honor substituted. "Is Phillip
here?" She looked expectantly around the
great hall, subconsciously noting the dark
wood against cream walls, the high vaulted
ceilings.

"No, he has gone —"

Honor felt his presence before he spoke
from behind her. "I'll handle this, Mama
Rosa."

The Mexican woman opened her lips to
protest, but Honor was already whirling
toward the doorway behind her. "Phillip!"
Her greeting fell to a whisper. *"What has
happened to you?"* Her horrified eyes took in

the bloodstained bandage around his head, the way he leaned against the wall for support. "Darling, my dream was true. You're hurt!"

"It's all right," he caught her in midflight, before she could throw her arms around him. "Mama Rosa, can you get me something for this? That ornery colt Juan and I were working with stumbled and threw me against the corner of the fence."

Mama Rosa came to life and scuttled away, but Honor clung to Phillip. "You must sit down." She spied a blanket-covered couch against the opposite wall and half led him there. "Oh, Phillip, I just knew something terrible had happened. That's why I got here so early."

The man on the couch looked at her wearily. "You call me Phillip. I don't seem to have had the pleasure of meeting you."

Honor stared at him, unable to believe her own ears. "Not know me! You mean you don't remember the canyon — or anything?"

He passed his hand over his eyes. "I don't seem to. Would you mind terribly? Could we talk later?"

Her face reflected how stricken her soul was, but she only said slowly, "You mean the blow on the head has erased everything

— you really don't know who I am?"

Her agony must have shown. The dull eyes looked sympathetic. "I'm sorry." He turned toward Mama Rosa, who had come in with basin and antiseptic. "Mama Rosa, give this young lady a room — what did you say your name was?"

"Honor Brooks."

Phillip staggered to his feet. "I'll talk with you later, Miss Brooks. Wait here until Mama finishes with me, and she'll show you where to go." He lurched against her, then with Mama as guide, disappeared into another room, leaving Honor alone.

She sank to the couch, automatically smoothing the blanket. What a horrible thing to have happen! What should she do? Phillip looked so ghastly with that bloody bandage on his head, not at all like the man she had known. Yet a great sympathy went through her. How must he feel, being hurt and entering his home to find a perfect stranger there, one who called him "darling" and insisted he knew her?

She sprang to her feet. Why was she standing there doing nothing? Couldn't she help? But before she could more than take a step in the direction he had gone, Mama Rosa came back. "Come with me, please." She led the way up a curved staircase and into a room at the right. "You will stay here."

"But how is he?"

Mama Rosa's impassive face widened in a smile. "He is fine. It is nothing for him to be thrown. Now he needs rest. He will see you after siesta." She threw back the covers of the huge carved bed so in keeping with the other decor. "Rest. I will tell you when to come." The smile came again. "But first I bring you a tamale."

"Thank you, Mama Rosa." The door had closed behind her. Honor smiled. Even in his pain Phillip must have thought of her. The plate Mama Rosa brought contained not only tamales, but a taco as well, bearing little resemblance to the pale imitations Honor had eaten in San Francisco. She drank glasses of ice water to get the heat from her mouth, then threw herself onto the bed. If siesta was the custom here, she was all for it.

After the sleepless night, the good food and warm room had done its work well. She slept until slanting afternoon sun rays filled the room. She had only stirred enough to torpidly reach for her shoes when Mama Rosa tapped at the partly open door. "Come now."

Honor ran a brush through her hair and

followed the Mexican woman down a long hall, carpeted in red, to the open door of a large room. "You go in there." Mama Rosa stood aside.

Why should she feel strangely unwilling to cross the threshold? For a moment she hesitated, then the rich voice she had learned to love called, "Come in."

She stepped inside, glancing quickly toward Phillip. He was not lying down as she had expected. He was seated behind the most massive desk she had ever seen. This must be the study. It had all the stark necessities of a business office: typewriter, file cabinets, everything needed to proclaim it the utilitarian room it was. Honor bit back her disappointment. Even if he didn't remember her, did he have to fortify himself behind that desk? It was as she had feared and more. He was not only unapproachable, he was totally remote from anything connected with her.

She could delay looking at him no longer. To her relief the bandage had given way to a smaller patch near his hairline. He still looked pale, but it could be the filtered light through heavy drapes.

Phillip leaned toward her, motioning her to a chair at the end of the desk. "Miss Brooks, this must come as quite a shock to you. You don't know how sorry I am."

"It is a shock, Phillip." Could that strained voice really be hers? "After the past few weeks, all our plans —" she faltered. How could she talk to the stonefaced man across the desk?

The measured glance softened. Abruptly Phillip rose and walked to her. "I believe we should go somewhere a little more relaxed. You were right. I remember nothing of you, but I want to know." His kindness nearly broke her control. She stumbled a bit, and he caught her arm as they walked downstairs and into the courtyard. Blinded by tears, she was only barely aware of its beauty. His strong hold was all that mattered.

"Now." He seated her on a garden bench, pillowed with cushions, sheltered by a great cottonwood tree. "Tell me all about us."

For a moment Honor was speechless. "But — how can I tell you — it's like talking with a stranger! Oh, Phillip, can't you remember any of it?" A new thought struck her. "Not even knowing me in San Francisco?"

"San Francisco!" For a moment hope flared, but died as Phillip shook his head. "No. I remember nothing of the sort." He must have sensed her distress. "Talk to me not as a stranger, but as a friend. I promise not to interrupt."

It was the most bizarre assignment Honor could have been given. To tell Phillip, beloved, yet not knowing her, how they met — everything!

Honor was aware of the strong clasp of his hand as she leaned back on the bench. Hastily she sketched in their meeting and friendship in San Francisco. She skipped over the sorrow during Granny and Keith's deaths and looking for a job, and went into how the Stones hired her and brought her to the Grand Canyon. Now and then he smiled, giving her courage to go on. After all, this man had fallen in love with her and proposed, even inviting her to Casa del Sol. Why should she fear him simply because he could not remember through no fault of his own?

When she reached the part about meeting again at the canyon she was breathless, glad for the lengthening shadows hiding his face and her own. "I ran for the door, crossed the lobby, started upstairs. I could hear laughing voices. The next moment I was on the floor, staring up stupidly. You had been talking with Babs and the rest of them. You picked me up, recognized me." A soft glow filled her face. "You said, 'I say, I've knocked you down with my clumsiness. I should have been looking where I was going.' "

There was a muffled sound of protest from Phillip. She continued, "It was the beginning of — of an old acquaintance."

"And love?" His stern voice gave her the shivers.

"Yes," she whispered. "What we felt in San Francisco when you asked me to wait for you all came back. As the days passed, and we spent time together at the canyon —" Her voice trailed off. She returned to the present with an effort. "You invited the Stones and me to visit Casa del Sol. You wanted to prepare your brother before we arrived. I have to confess, I am anxious to meet him. He's grown to be something of an ogre in my mind." She laughed nervously.

As if galvanized into action, Phillip leaped to his feet to tower over her. She was instantly contrite. "I'm sorry! It's just that I want him to like me. When will I meet him?"

"Soon enough. Go on. The Stones couldn't make it?"

"No. He was called home. Is this bringing anything back to you?" She could hear him breathing hard. He shook his head and said,

"I promised not to interrupt, but I have to tell you I know this isn't easy for you. Believe me, it's the only way."

She gave a little cry and put her other hand over his. "I'm so glad you understand! Last night I dreamed, strange, troubled hands reaching toward me. I woke up feeling something terrible had happened to you. That's why I came early."

He released her hands and drew her closer. "I don't think it's terrible. I think perhaps it's the best thing that ever happened."

"What a strange remark! Are you sure your head is all right?"

"It's fine." He stood, propelled to his feet with almost catlike grace. "Honor, we must have dinner. You can finish telling me the story later. We'll build a fire in the fireplace."

After the delicious dinner Mama Rosa served on a tray in her room, Honor followed the housekeeper downstairs to what evidently was the library. It was all she had pictured, with its blazing fire. Again she was grateful for the darkness.

"Honor, the one thing you haven't told me is how you feel. Are you in love with me? Did you promise to marry me?"

Her shining hair curtained her downcast face. "Yes."

She could hear the sharp intake of breath before Phillip answered. "And you're the kind of girl who would never go back on a promise." It was not a question, but a statement. It brought Honor's eyes to his.

"I am bound by my word." For one frightening moment she was back on the canyon's edge, facing the storm overhead and the tumult in her heart. It was almost as if she were being given a second chance to reconsider. Phillip didn't remember her. What if he never did? What if she was deliberately deluding herself into thinking she could be queen of this near-palace? The immensity of the very room in which they sat increased her doubts. What was she, a child's governess, doing in this place?

"Well?"

Even as she opened her mouth to break the chains binding her to this unknown Phillip, memory of her position came. Granny, Keith, home — all gone.

Even the security of her position with the Stones was gone. She could not go back. What did it matter if he didn't know her now? When he remembered he would still be her beloved, the man who was kind to Heather, who openly confessed a past dark with unsaid choices but who also reached forward to a brighter future here on the ranch with her to strengthen him.

"You really think Phillip Travis is the husband you need?"

Had he divined her thoughts, or was his memory returning? "Yes." Once it was said, it was easier. "We will share our lives, create a home, have children — just as we planned." It was all she could get out for now.

Phillip broke away, turned to the fire and moodily stared into the flames. "Go home, Honor. Back to San Francisco. You will never find happiness here."

His command roused a demon of opposition she hadn't known lay within. "Never! You asked me to marry you. I accepted. Surely you will remember in a few days."

"Have you ever been in love before?" He swung to face her.

"Once." She could feel a reminiscent smile turn to laughter as she confessed, "A certain soldier came to San Francisco — he asked me to wait for him." She sobered. "When he didn't write, I shut my heart and wouldn't admit how it hurt."

"Phillip Travis?"

"Yes."

He gripped her shoulders. "Are you prepared to deal with drinking, sometimes to excess? With other women?"

Her confidence turned to fear. "But —

but you said I was the one you'd waited for all your life. You said drinking didn't mean anything when I was with you."

"And you still want to marry me?" Disbelief filled his eyes. "Even knowing those protestations might not be true?" His face suddenly iced over. "Or do you expect me to change?"

"I — I hope you will!" Stung by the agony inside she cried, "Why do you downgrade yourself? I know there is a part of you that wants more from life than idleness." She faced him squarely and had the satisfaction of seeing him drop his eyes.

"Did we talk about this at the canyon?"

She had to be honest. "Some. You told me I was seeing the best of you there, alone, away from temptation. I want to help you, Phillip."

"What else did we talk about?"

"Everything. Your desire to be more part of the ranch, to convince your brother —" She broke off.

She wasn't prepared for the fury in the blazing eyes threatening to scorch her or his low reply, "Forget about my brother!"

"Phillip!"

He ignored her cry. His eyes turned to black coals. "If you expect to have all your childish fantasies come true, you better keep moving. Phillip Travis is not a knight on a white horse."

She swayed, unconsciously putting up her hands in protest. "Why do you keep referring to yourself so? Or are you pretending? Maybe you do remember." Horror filled her. "That's it, isn't it? You do remember and are regretting getting entangled with a governess." Her face felt tight, her lips parched. "You have changed. Did Babs convince you I wasn't worthy? When you prate to me of worth, is it me you are thinking of, *or yourself?*"

He sidestepped the question and gripped her shoulders again until she knew there would be bruises in the morning. "Is there nothing I can say that will make you go away?"

"Only that you never want to see me again." One final time she felt on the brink, but she ignored the bridge and plunged in. "Nothing else on earth can make me leave you."

Phillip's face twisted, a groan escaped his tightly clenched lips. "Then stay — and may heaven protect you!"

Even through her victory the bitter drop remained. She had forfeited the right to expect God's protection — for Phillip. Shaken, she pushed down the thought and lightened the atmosphere. "I expect you to show me Arizona. Not just Casa del Sol, but the White Mountains and the Oak Creek Canyon and —"

"And just when are we getting married in all this?"

Honor caught her breath. "Oh, not until you remember everything, and you will."

"I am already getting a clearer picture of the past from what you have said."

Joy skyrocketed inside her as she lifted her face and put her arms around him in a gesture both loving and protective. "Then let's do as we planned. We can ride and talk and learn to really know each other!" She was amazed at her own boldness and dropped her arms hastily. "Phillip, you seem almost a different person here in your own home, almost a stranger."

She could feel his surprise as he asked. "Which man do you love? The vacationer at the canyon, or the rancher in his home?"

"Since it will be my home, too, it will have to be the rancher —" She never finished. Slowly he crushed her to him, seeking her lips with his own. Her arms crept around his neck as she returned his kiss. "Why, Phillip, you really are a stranger! You have never kissed me like that before." She pulled back and stared at him.

"A man in his castle is a different creature than on any other ground." A curious glint filled his eyes, and the lips that had claimed hers turned upward into a smile she did not understand. But when he held out his arms again, she flew to them like a homing pigeon. Stranger or not, Phillip Travis was the man she loved.

5

Somewhere in the darkness a horse softly whinnied. Honor turned in the heavily carved bed, then ran to the window. Why would anyone be out now? Moonlight sneaked through her slightly parted drapes to touch a clock on the wall. One-thirty.

Her eyes widened as she pushed the heavy drapes open. A tall rider was swinging easily onto the back of a white horse that gleamed in the moonlight. His upturned face brought a gasp to Honor's lips. Phillip! The prancing horse daintily stepped away from the corral and down the path. Honor could hear the rhythm of hooves as horse and rider gradually increased speed once away from the hacienda.

"How strange! I didn't think Phillip would be the type to go riding at midnight." A thrill shot through Honor as she shivered her way back to bed. The night was crisp, and fresh air streamed through the partially opened window. She breathed deep and hugged her knees. It all smelled so clean, pines and flowers. How could she be so fortunate?

A smile lit her face in the darkness,

sending a glow through her. The next instant it vanished in a frown. How different Phillip was in his own home! Why had he ordered her back to San Francisco? She could feel her heartbeat quicken. He could not be the selfish person he had described, or he wouldn't be putting her ahead of himself. Even though he seemed firmer and stronger here at Casa del Sol, he must have been thinking of her happiness, afraid he could not fill her expectations. A protective wave of love for him replaced her other feelings. She would help him be what she believed he could be — in spite of his own protestations. No one could feel about the canyon the way Phillip did and yet be narrow-minded enough not to recognize a better way of life than that of his friends.

The weakness of her reasoning hit her immediately. She refused to listen to the voice inside. She had chosen. She would not turn back. She would become mistress of Casa del Sol. The high ceilings of the spacious room echoed her whisper, "Is it all a dream?" She pinched her arm hard, then rubbed the aching spot. No. She really was here. In her wildest dreams she had only imagined visiting a large ranch someday. Now she would be part of it, and when Phillip's brother came — Honor's face flamed in the darkness. Where was he? She hadn't even thought to ask. How could she have blurted out as she had about Phillip's brother being an ogre? Phillip must think her gauche if not downright rude. She set her chin resolutely. When he did come, she would make him like her. Much of her happiness depended on the unknown stranger.

Now that she had seen Casa del Sol she should be able to conjure up a better image of Phillip's brother than an ogre! He must be industrious. Phillip had confessed indolence, and the ranch still prospered. Her fingers interlaced as she promised the night wind, "Phillip is going to learn to work. He will be happier. I'll start by asking to see the ranch. He can't help learning when he sees how interested I am."

Honor shivered. "Learning! Will I ever learn everything there is to know about this place? Will I ever really be comfortable with Mama Rosa? She will have to teach me." She laughed nervously. "Nothing in my background has fitted me for this!"

Memory of the mule trip and resulting stiffness brought a rueful twist to her good intentions. "I'll have to learn to ride. Not on that magnificent white animal I just saw. Maybe there's a pony."

Her thoughts returned to the absent

brother. No picture would come. Sleepy from her mental gymnastics, she turned over, wondering where Phillip had gone.

A gentle tapping roused her. The brilliance of the sun pouring through the drapes she had left open hurt her eyes for a moment.

"Come in." She pulled the sheet up under her chin, stealing a glance at the clock. Ten! She had slept away half the morning of her first day at Casa del Sol.

"I brought your breakfast." Rosa's brown face above the tray was as impassive as it had been the day before.

Honor smiled warmly, noting it brought a response. The muscles in Rosa's face relaxed. "Good morning, Rosa. What a beautiful day!" She slipped from bed and into a robe and slippers, then ran to the window again. She looked down, amazed at the pang that shot through her when she discovered the corral was empty.

"Where are the horses? And Phillip? I heard him ride out last night."

Rosa's gaze was startled and there was a slight breathiness in her reply. "Felipe is not here."

"And his brother?"

"Senor is not here, either."

Honor whirled. "You sound —" She

broke off. It was not for her to comment on how Rosa sounded. "This looks delicious, but I can never eat it all!"

For the first time Rosa actually smiled. "You will eat. Casa del Sol makes you hungry." She fussed about, buttering the hot biscuits, rearranging the silver. "The peaches come from our own trees. The bacon is from our hogs. The honey is from our hives."

"Rosa." Honor put her hand on the sturdy brown one. "I'm going to marry Phillip, but I don't know anything about running a place such as this! I can cook, but not like this. Will you teach me all I should know?"

The smile became a beam, then faded. "It will be for Senor to say."

"Senor?" Honor was puzzled, then light broke. "Oh, you mean Phillip's brother." Something of her fear of the unknown Senor showed in her flat voice.

"Si." Rosa moved toward the door. "Call when you have eaten." She indicated an old-fashioned bell pull. Dignified, with no trace of the softer nature she had shown only moments before, Rosa opened the door and glided through.

"Very much the controlling influence of Casa del Sol, " Honor told the empty room. "She changed when I mentioned my new brother-to-be. She calls him Senor. He must be *uno grande hombre*." Honor laughed at her own mixture of Latin and Spanish. "If I'm going to use any Spanish I'd better learn more than I know now!"

The breakfast was delicious, and when she had finished Honor bathed and dressed, this time in a simple blue gown. She would carry her own tray downstairs. Perhaps Rosa would be a little friendlier. But it wasn't Rosa Honor found when she finally located the kitchen after opening three doors to other rooms. Phillip sat at the gleaming white-topped table so out of keeping with the rest of the house.

"Good morning, Phillip." The pleats in her skirt swung as she started toward him.

He motioned her back. "Don't get too close. I've been with the horses and am not fit to be around beautiful ladies."

Color flowed freely into her face. He sounded like a little boy. "I saw you ride out last night. Where did you go?"

"I had a lot to think of." Laughter fled from his voice. His dark eyes held her as he pushed back his chair abruptly. "How about a ride this morning? You have breakfasted, haven't you?"

"So much I probably won't be able to get on a horse!"

Her fears were unfounded. Phillip led out a pinto pony a half hour later. Clad in knickers and boots, with her khaki skirt and a sombrero borrowed from Rosa's daughter, Carlotta, she managed to get in the saddle with one gentle boost from Phillip. Her pony, Jingles, had an easy gait. Phillip said Jingles was a single-footer. It was almost like riding a rocking horse!

Honor reined her in at the top of a cedar-covered ridge. "Does it never end?" Her eyes ranged from the red and white shorthorns grazing the valley floor to the already-snowcapped mountains to the north. Casa del Sol's roof shone red in the sunlight, warming the gray sage and green pines and cedars surrounding it.

"It is a responsibility," Phillip said. "A trust from my grandfather and father." Honor sensed he spoke more to himself than to her. "Dozens of families depend on us and the way this ranch is run. Not just our cowboys and other workers. We furnish meat for a lot of Arizona."

"I believe it. It's almost too much for one family."

"That's what my brother says." Phillip's eyes were somber.

A strange feeling dimmed the sun streaming down on them. He couldn't mean his brother was considering selling the ranch! Not just when she had determined to make Phillip part of it. She started to speak, thought better of it, and said, "I just hope I can be —"

She never finished the sentence. A man on a horse was racing toward them, yellow paper in his hand.

Honor looked at Phillip. His face was the color of parchment. He spurred his horse, and the white stallion leaped forward. Flying hooves ate up the distance between the two men. Honor started to follow. She was struck by the rigidity of Phillip's figure as he took the yellow paper and read it. She automatically hesitated, and Phillip turned back toward her. As he shortened the space between them she couldn't help admiring the ease with which he rode.

The parchment color had left his face, replaced by a dark flush. "Honor, would you marry me right away? Before the end of the week?"

"But we agreed —"

"I know. I just don't feel that way any longer. You don't want a big fancy wedding, do you?"

"No, Phillip." She had a terrifying sense of something lurking ahead, some unknown danger. "I just want a simple ceremony. But

I wanted more time, time for you to re-member —" Her voice gave way.

"I know." He touched his mount's side lightly with his heels, bringing him along-side Jingles. "I'll take care of you, Honor. I'll make sure you don't come to any harm. Won't you do as I ask?"

Honor's eyes dropped to the yellow page still in Phillip's hand. Sudden under-standing filled her.

Phillip's eyes followed her gaze. "Yes, it's from my brother. He will be home some-time next week."

Honor couldn't bear the way his head drooped, as if in shame. A great wave of love and understanding again flooded her. Phillip needed her. He dreaded the home-coming, what might happen. Would there be violent objections? The same protective warmth that had stirred the night before crept into her veins. If disappointment min-gled with it, she valiantly pushed it back. Did it really matter if she knew this white-faced man weeks, months, or years? Again she squelched the mighty *yes* her conscience was shouting. If Phillip needed her so much, how could she refuse? "The only white dress I have is one I made from a dis-card of Mrs. Stone's wardrobe."

"You don't think that matters!" He swept

her into his arms. It was enough to eliminate any lingering doubt she might have had.

On the way home Honor was quiet. Phillip did not attempt to intrude on her thoughts. It wasn't until he helped her down that he said, "Honor, no matter what happens, you won't ever despise me, will you?"

He knows I know he's weak. Honor bit back a betraying rush of tears. "I will love you as long as I live."

Phillip did not kiss her again. Instead he held her close to his rapidly beating heart. "It's the only way. When you understand, when —"

"I already understand." She placed gloved fingers over his lips.

"Rest a bit before lunch, Honor. This Arizona weather is far different from what you are used to in San Francisco."

"I noticed I had a little trouble breathing."

"We're several thousand feet high. You'll adjust in a few days."

Honor ran upstairs. In just a few days she would be Phillip's wife — for better or worse. Why did that phrase have to pop up? She whirled into her room.

Carlotta, in a school skirt and middy blouse, looked up from folding back the bedspread. Her Spanish ancestry shone in her shining dark hair and eyes. "How do you like Casa del Sol?"

"I don't know if I can ever be worthy of it."

She repeated the words later that week to Phillip. They had ridden through the soft twilight to a different knoll above the valley. "This place — can I ever be worthy of it?"

"Worthy — you? It is I —" He broke off, unseeing eyes tracing the pattern of a bubbling stream in the valley that was only a silver thread from their viewpoint.

"You will be worthy, too, Phillip. When your brother comes, we'll tell him you want to really be part of the ranch. He will respect your feelings."

Phillip's dark eyes flashed. "The ogre, as you nicknamed him?"

Honor turned beet red. "I'm sorry for that. I really didn't mean it. It's just that I want us to be happy here —" The wistfulness in her voice brought a squeeze from Phillip's hand that threatened to crush her fingers, even in the sturdy riding gloves Carlotta had furnished.

"I pray you will never be anything here but happy."

"Just to think that a few weeks ago Mr. Stone was telling me not to come down here and marry some Arizonan!" She laughed.

"Would you rather have waited and asked

him to the wedding?" Honor felt the tension in the question.

"No. He would never understand how I could be so sure so quickly, when for all my life I've been waiting." Her fiery color intensified until it matched the jutting rocks near where they had stopped. "I'm not sure I understand myself."

"You aren't regretting it?"

There was no hesitation. "No, Phillip. I will never regret marrying you tomorrow."

"You're the sweetest thing on earth." He leaned across from his horse Sol's back to kiss her, almost reverently. "I will do everything in my power to keep you from regretting it." His eyes were like glittering obsidian in a chalky face. "Honor, will you promise to trust me, no matter what?"

"I will."

Even later, as she dressed for her last hours as a single woman, Honor thought of the scene on the little plateau. Tomorrow she would take her wedding vows. But her real vow had been taken on that little plateau overlooking Casa del Sol.

"This time tomorrow I'll be your wife." Honor's eyes were pools of happiness as Phillip walked her to her door that night. The moonlit night threw patterns of fantastic beauty across the upper hall.

"Yes." Why did Phillip seem distracted?

"You — you aren't regretting?"

She felt him start in the dimness. "I regret nothing." He captured her, kissing her the way he had done the first night she arrived at Casa del Sol. Honor's doubts fled before the intensity of his love. It was a long time before she broke away.

"Good night, Phillip." She slipped through the heavy door, closing it behind her. Just before it shut out all sounds, somewhere in the hacienda a bell rang. The telephone? What if Phillip's brother — she laughed at her own fancies. How melodramatic to think a disapproving man would appear on the doorstep at the eleventh hour to stop her wedding!

At last Honor had time to think.

Tomorrow Juan and Rosa and Carlotta would go to Flagstaff for her wedding with Phillip. Carlotta would be her bridesmaid. Phillip had said earlier this evening he had arranged for them to be married by a minister.

Her heart swelled. How thoughtful! He had instinctively known how she would want it. A horrendous thought marred her happiness.

What if Phillip's brother should be in Flagstaff?

She punched her pillow, then buried her face in its cooling depths. She must get over this obsession about the man! All she knew about him was the little Phillip had told her.

Again Honor heard hooves in the night and ran to her window. Again she saw the tall, dark-haired man mount an unsaddled white horse, one she now knew as Sol. Was he nervous about tomorrow? The thought was strangely comforting. She had been so sure she'd never sleep. Now she dove into bed and moments later was unconscious.

"Senorita, you are beautiful!" There was no disapproving silence about Rosa this morning. "Senora Dolores would be proud to have you marry her son!"

Honor's eyes filled. Early this morning a large box had arrived and a note from Phillip:

I KNOW YOU HAVE A
WHITE DRESS TO BE
MARRIED IN. I HOPE YOU
WILL WEAR THIS WITH IT.

There had been no signature, but inside had been the most exquisitely wrought lace mantilla Honor had ever seen or imagined.

Slightly yellowed with age, it only brought out the highlights in her skin.

"I don't know how to wear it," she confessed to Carlotta.

"We will help you," the beautiful bridesmaid promised, dark face picking up color from the soft rosy gown she wore. Now as Honor faced herself in the mirror, it was not only her own image she saw but the joy on the faces of Rosa and Carlotta. Turning impulsively she threw her arms around them both, heedless of the priceless mantilla. "I am so glad I came to Arizona!"

"We are glad, too! You and Senor will be very happy." Carlotta's eyes danced

"We will help you dress and arrange the mantilla when we get to Flagstaff," Rosa promised as they disrobed her and carefully packed her dress and mantilla in boxes. "Bad luck for bridegroom to see you in dress before wedding."

"Mamacita believes in old customs." Carlotta laughed, but there was genuine respect and love in her voice.

"I think I do, too." Honor danced to the window, still in her long white slip. "Was there ever a more beautiful day for a bride? I'm a fall person. You know, my birthday is next week."

Rosa beamed. "Why did you not wait and

be married on your birthday?"

"Phillip didn't want to wait so long." Her voice was muffled in her slip as she quickly drew on a simple dress for the drive into Flagstaff. "I think he's a little bit afraid of his brother coming home and stopping the wedding."

In the absolute silence that fell Honor pulled the top triumphantly over her head and settled it. Only then did she realize how still it had become. She was instantly contrite! "I shouldn't have said that! It is just that I want us all to be happy, and I wish he *would* come!"

Rosa's sober glance reminded Honor of the way she had responded when Honor first came. Quietly she gathered up the slip and packed it, then turned toward the door. "Senor Travis is a fine man." She slipped out, leaving Honor staring.

"It's all right." Carlotta seemed anxious to bridge the uncomfortable moment. "Mamacita thinks the sun doesn't come up or go down without first consulting Senor!"

Honor laughed in spite of feeling guilty, picturing the sun bowing daily before Casa del Sol and asking permission to rise and set! "Just where is he now?" Honor inquired as she ran a brush through her hair.

"Oh, here and there." Carlotta sounded

vague, disinclined to discuss his whereabouts. "Where are you going for your honeymoon — or do you know?"

"Right here. Where could there be anything more glorious?" She spun about and frowned. "When we were at the canyon we talked about going back after we were married. Carlotta, it's so strange. He still doesn't seem to remember a lot of what happened at the canyon."

"Why is it important?" The liquid brown eyes shifted.

Honor turned back to the window, noting how the golden leaves fluttered — cottonwood, aspen, birch. She had learned to love them all. "He just seems so much older here. Different. More mature."

The watching eyes reflected breathlessness in Carlotta's question. "Which do you love more? The canyon man, or this one?"

Honor's face glowed. "I love the man who owns Casa del Sol. More than anything in the world."

"Then I suggest you come with me and marry him." The laughing invitation from the doorway brought consternation to Carlotta's face until she saw Honor light up and bow. "I'll do just that."

"You like my invitation, senorita?" The watching dark eyes were suddenly sober.

"I love your invitation, senor." She turned to Carlotta. "Coming?"

"No. Mamacita and Papa and I will take our own car. You will want to come back alone." Her flashing smile added to her beauty.

"That's right, Carlotta. I'm going to want my wife all to myself for a few hours!"

Honor could feel a tiny pulse beating in her throat. "You'll bring everything, Carlotta?"

"Everything."

Carlotta was as good as her word. A few hours later she carefully lifted the priceless mantilla to Honor's head. But it was for Rosa to carefully adjust its folds so it cascaded to Honor's shoulders. Something in Honor's eyes seemed to touch the good woman's heart. "Be happy, senorita." She pressed her warm brown cheek to Honor's paler one, feeling the clutch of nervous fingers before Honor laughed.

"It is time." Carlotta threw open the door of the little room next to the chapel.

How could Phillip have arranged so much in such a short time? The small chapel seemed smothered with autumn leaves, dark fir branches. Fall flowers of every color perfumed the room. The measured tones of the Wedding March from *Lohengrin* softly pulsated, keeping time to Honor's beating heat.

Honor clutched her bouquet of old-fashioned flowers. They must have been especially chosen by Phillip from those she admired most in his courtyard. Late roses, even a few tiny forget-me-nots. It was a shame for such a perfect wedding to be seen by so few.

Carlotta's rosy skirt swished to a standstill. It was Honor's turn. Shakily, she started down the long aisle, seeing nothing except Phillip waiting for her.

The wedding ceremony was a little blurred. Only one thing really stood out in the kaleidoscope of Honor's memory. When the minister turned to Phillip he said, "Do you, James Travis, take this woman . . ."

Honor gasped, feeling as if inchworms were measuring her spine. The next moment Phillip's strong hand tightened reassuringly on her own. His face was pale, but the dark eyes were steady. Honor wondered how the minister could have made such a mistake. Obviously it was all right, or Phillip would have stopped the service for a correction. Her surprise soon settled down. Of course — James must be Phillip's first name and necessary for legal documents.

Her unanswered musings were drowned in the "I do" that rang from the arched beams of the little chapel.

Honor's own response was quieter. Two words, so little to signify passing her life into James Phillip Travis's keeping until death did them part. She blinked back mist that hid the scene for a moment, realizing as never before how truly irrevocable that promise was.

"I pronounce you man and wife. What God hath joined together, let no man put asunder." In spite of her joy, Honor shivered. How could any man or woman break promises as solemn as the vows in the wedding service?

Phillip turned to her. His lips found hers, lingering as if loath to let her go. She could feel his resignation when he finally released her. Her heart responded. Their first kiss as man and wife; holy, beautiful. If only everyone would just go away and leave them alone! But it was not to be. From somewhere a photographer appeared.

"I thought you would want pictures," her new husband explained. "But not during the actual ceremony. I've seen too many weddings interrupted by photographers. Would you mind posing with me, Mrs. Travis?"

"Not a bit, Mr. Travis." Excitement like a

skyrocket trembled within her as she laughed and smiled. Phillip had even arranged for a wedding cake in a nearby restaurant's private room. "We want pictures for our children." He watched her color rise as she stammered.

"It's a bit hard to talk to a brand new husband, isn't it?" She finally gave up small talk efforts in total honesty.

"It's also time for us to go home."

"Home!" Something golden glowed within Honor. "House of the Sun. May it ever prove to be so for us."

"And when the shadows come?"

She looked resolutely into his face. "We will know the sun is always there. Shadows pass, the sun returns."

"You darling!" The ardent look in his eyes stirred her. But he only said, "Wouldn't you like to change into something else for the drive back? That mantilla must be heavy."

Honor thought for a moment. "I'll take the mantilla off, but leave my gown on. I won't ever have another wedding day, so I want to look beautiful on this one."

He gently lifted the mantilla from her hair and handed it to Mama Rosa, voice sober. "Put it away, Mama. I'm taking Honor home."

"Vaya con Dios." The beautiful Spanish blessing rested on them as Phillip helped her into the big touring car. She waved and smiled as they backed and turned.

"What does it mean, Phillip? Something about God, I know that."

"Go with God."

"How fitting. *Vaya con Dios.*" She repeated the words, then turned back to him. "Phillip, it will take all the days of our lives to learn what there is to know about each other."

The Willys swerved, righted itself, then slowly inched ahead. Honor vaguely noticed and wondered at a honking carload of people next to them, waiting for a wagon ahead to pass, but paid little attention to them. Phillip's hands were white on the wheel. "Honor, there's something I have to tell you, as soon as we get home —"

His sentence was never finished. From the open Stutz next to them a wild whoop went up. Staring across at the other car, Honor was stunned. A tall dark-haired man was wildly waving — and he was an exact replica of Phillip!

She opened her lips to speak, then glanced at Phillip. He had gone a curious color, as if all the blood had drained from his face under the tan. His lips twisted. The pain in his face caught at her heart. Again she tried to speak, but nothing came from her frozen throat. Was Phillip that much afraid of his brother? It must be he in the other car, but why hadn't Phillip told her they were twins?

Her calculations, slowed by shock, were shattered when the other man called, his mocking voice clearly audible in the late fall air. "Well, Honor, James — what have you two been up to? And Honor in a white dress, even!"

Honor reeled back against the seat. It was the same voice she had heard on the floor of El Tovar Hotel. There was no mistaking it — the man in that car was Phillip Travis! Arm about Babs, laughing with the others Honor knew from the canyon, he was in curious contrast to the man gripping the steering wheel of the car she was in — the man she had just promised to love, honor, and cherish for as long as she lived.

"That's Phillip." Her voice broke in a sob, pleading for understanding, just as that same something that had haunted her during the wedding magnified. "But then, who, what — he called you James. You aren't, you can't be —" She couldn't get another sound past the mountain that seemed to have closed off her throat.

Her words seemed to release her companion from the trance they had fallen into, almost as if a wicked spell had been called out in that laughing, accusing voice from the other car.

He turned to her for an instance, then shot ahead and around the corner out of sight of the pointing, laughing hecklers. A crooked smile touched his ashen lips, a mocking salute recognized her stumbling question. "Meet James Travis, senora. Once again the lovely princess has married the ogre."

6

"*You?* It can't be true." Honor flexed stiff lips, sliding far away from him, as if he really were an ogre. Flecks of memory darted to her. "Then —" Her laugh was slightly hysterical. "Of course. That's why you didn't remember anything from the canyon. *Because you never were there with me!*"

His silence was maddening. Honor swallowed hard. It must be a nightmare. Her perfect wedding, and now this? Impossible. The man beside her who had been so gentle, so loving — an imposter. She could feel herself shrinking into nothingness. In self-defense she lashed out. "How could you do such a thing? Telling me you were Phillip? Making me fall in love with you?"

"But my dear." James seemed grimly amused. "*You* were the one to call me Phillip. If you remember, I never once told you I was Phillip. Why should I? If you will remember a little more, I tried to send you away. I told you the truth. I told you Phillip Travis could never make you happy. I also told you that your childish longing for someone to come along on a white horse did not fit Phillip."

112

Honor moistened her parched lips with the tip of her tongue. In minutes the companionable man she had known since she arrived at the ranch had changed into a stranger. "Then I was right. You were a stranger when I arrived at Casa del Sol. You were nothing like Phillip."

"Thank you." This time he laughed aloud. "That's the finest compliment you could give me."

"But why?" She had to break through his calm. "Why did you marry me?"

"There was no other choice." His laughing mask slipped. In its place was a deadly serious man. "I had to protect you from my dear brother. I tried to send you away, and you wouldn't go. I tried to tell you about him, and you wouldn't listen. So —"

"So you passed yourself off as Phillip and hurried up the wedding before he came!" She fumbled for the door handle as they neared another corner. "I'm getting out of here and now!"

"You aren't going anywhere." The strong arm she knew so well reached across, pinning her against the seat, infuriating her more. "Don't ever try and run away from me. This world isn't big enough for you to hide in."

"Who are you to tell me what I shall and shall not do?" Honor wrenched free and sat trembling as he picked up speed and headed onto the open road, leaving Flagstaff behind.

"I just happen to be your husband."

"Not for long! As soon as I can get help you won't be." Her voice gathered assurance. "Phillip will never stand for this. He will come to Casa del Sol for me."

"He will be welcome — so long as he remembers you are my wife."

"Your wife? Are you insane? Do you think I'd stay with you after what you have done?"

"Of course." Could that really be surprise in his face as he shot a keen glance at her. "You told me you were truthful and steadfast. You told me you never broke a vow. You also promised to love, honor, and cherish me until death parted us. How can you be ready so soon to break those vows?"

If sheer fury could kill, James Travis would have died on the spot. "You don't by any stretch of imagination think those vows are valid under these circumstances! I believe you are insane! I was right. You *are* an ogre!"

To her amazement, James threw his head back and laughed. Didn't any of this bother him at all? She would show him! She would get away at the first opportunity!

The slow, mocking voice went on. "Really, Honor, don't you believe in fate, or God, or something? I would have bet you do. How do you know this wasn't all planned?"

"How dare you? Isn't it enough that you have ruined my life? How can you mock God?" A tiny drum beat in her brain. *Isn't that what you've done?*

James whipped the car into a leafy lane out of sight of the main road, killed the motor, and turned to her. His face was as white as her own. The hands he placed on her shoulders dug in. "Ruined your life! Shall I tell you what your life would be like with your precious Phillip?"

"No! You have no right to malign your brother!"

The steel fingers bit deeper. It was all Honor could do to keep from crying out.

"It is not maligning to tell you the truth. You think you know Phillip Travis. You know nothing of him! You know only the front he puts on when he meets a new girl or woman. Do you think you are the first to be invited to Casa del Sol? No, not the first, nor the last. Babs is the only one he might ever be true to. When she is convinced of that, she will marry him. In the meantime, it is a succession of girls and women; summer, winter, fall, spring — season makes no difference. Phillip has the art of loving and leaving perfected to the highest degree." He gave her a little shake, his eyes burning like freshly stirred embers.

"Why didn't he meet you as he promised? Why didn't he come? I can tell you. Once he left the Grand Canyon you were only a dim memory." She flinched, and he shook her again. "Wake up, Honor. Do you think a man like Phillip could be true to you? Do you really think a man who loves women and carousing could settle down and make the kind of home you want, the kind of home you will have at Casa del Sol?"

"He promised to stop drinking! He said he didn't even want to drink when he was with me."

Slowly the fingers loosened. Terrible pity filled James's eyes as he pulled a newspaper from his pocket. "I hoped you would never have to see this."

Wordlessly, Honor took it. Blazoned across the front was a picture, unmistakably Phillip. His hair hung in his eyes, his mouth was slack. Underneath was the caption:

LOCAL RANCHER SPENDS NIGHT IN JAIL FOR DISORDERLY CONDUCT

The newspaper fell from Honor's nerveless fingers. "How could you be so cruel?"

"Is it more cruel to tell you the truth, or to let you marry him and find out for yourself?"

"But what am I to do?" All the old lack of self-confidence, of being totally alone, rushed over her. "You were joking when you said you expected me to stay, weren't you?"

James gripped her again, face chiseled in determination. "I never meant anything so much in my entire life."

She wrenched free. "To make the perfect touch, I suppose you're going to swear by all that's holy to you — or is anything? — that you fell in love with me at first sight and used this excuse to marry me."

Matching color burned in his face. "Why not? Didn't you do much the same with Phillip?" Speechless with fury, Honor couldn't reply. But James was not through. "Since you obviously wouldn't believe it, I won't swear undying love."

She hated him for the laughter underlying his thrust. "I wouldn't believe anything any Travis told me. You certainly planned it well. Why" — a new wave of indignation shot through her — "even Carlotta, Rosa — how could you get them to agree to such a monstrous pact? I should have known." Her eyes widened. "Rosa — she called Phillip 'Felipe.' She calls you 'Senor.' Why didn't I notice?"

"You were too busy deluding yourself about Phillip."

Honor buried her face in her hands, biting back a sob. She would not show weakness, not now.

"Cheer up, Honor. Things could be worse." James suddenly abandoned his lightness. "Don't hold it against Rosa and Carlotta. They knew you would be better off married to me, even hating me, than facing the inevitable humiliation you would find as Phillip's wife." His laugh sounded strained. "Who knows? We may even learn to love each other in time."

When Honor found her voice it came out in hard syllables, like crystal tears bouncing on a glassy surface. "That has to be the most ridiculous remark I have ever heard in my entire life. Love you? Never!"

"Never is a long time."

"You — you —" Her fury increased to the snapping point. In the midst of it a snatch of conversation with Carlotta burned red-hot in her mind. *Which do you love more? The canyon man, or this one?*

Her own reply now stood to accuse her. *I*

118

love the man who owns Casa del Sol — more than anything in the world.

"I demand you take me to the ranch so I can pack and go."

James laughed outright. "Wives don't leave their husbands so soon after the ceremony, my dear. Besides, I saw Phillip and his bunch pass the main road. They will be there to meet us. No one forced you to marry me, you know. If you remember, you even insisted —" He laughed again. "What a coup! Even Phillip will enjoy my trick, I'm sure the photographer will put our pictures in the paper. Perhaps there can be some more headlines about the Travis family:

YOUNG BEAUTIFUL BRIDE
MARRIES WRONG TWIN

How exciting! Something you can tell our children and grandchildren." Before Honor could find her tongue, he added casually, "It's lucky for me you are such an honorable person. Why, another woman might even do as you threatened and leave me. But not you." His face was blandly innocent as he put his foot on the gas and shot forward. "You are bound. Honor bound." She could have strangled him for his laugh. "You will go in looking like the bride you are."

Honor turned her back on him.

Never had miles gone by so slowly. All the glory of the day had gone. Even the red streaks heralding sunset failed to rouse Honor. James's laughing words had gone deep. In spite of everything he had done, she had promised, given her word. But how could she stay at Casa del Sol hating James as she now did? The love she had felt for Phillip was gone, obliterated by the sight of his drunken face in the newspaper. Deep inside a question formed — what if the love she had thought was for Phillip had really been for James at the ranch? She stepped on it, hard. She would never forgive him. Better to break her word than to remain where she had known so much happiness that had now turned to bitterness.

James must have read her thoughts. "Until you get over being upset, you needn't worry about my being around. I have work on the range and won't be in. You'll be treated as a special guest, nothing more."

Honor could feel color creeping up from the high neck of her wedding dress.

"I don't want a wife who still fancies herself in love with my twin brother. Until you get us sorted out in your mind you'll be just what I said, a special guest, nothing more."

Honor sank back against the seat, speechless again. What an unpredictable man! Yet his words had given birth to hope. What if she took him up on it? What if she stayed at Casa del Sol, let time help her decide what to do? She was in no condition to make any decisions right now. Too much had happened. She had been taken from joy to despair to disillusionment.

"You give your word?"

"I do." His warm hand shook her icy fingers in a businesslike grip as he swung into the cutoff toward Casa del Sol, as if a corporation merger had just been signed. "Now, let's show everyone what the partnership of Travis and Brooks-Travis can do. If they once find out you didn't know you married the wrong twin, this crowd will never let it be forgotten."

Wonder of wonders, Honor laughed. If she could just concentrate on getting through one thing at a time it would provide what she needed — a quiet place to think. But first she had to face that crowd — including Phillip. Phillip! How could such a terrible thing ever have happened? In love with one man, married to his twin brother who expected her to keep her vows. She shoved the thought aside. Now was not the time to think about it. She had to go in that house and face them all with a smile on her lips. With an involuntary shudder, she braced herself as James came to a stop, vaulted over the side of the low car, and before she knew what was happening scooped her up in his arms.

"Put me down," she ordered furiously, but he only grinned.

"It's what they'll expect! Hold still." With a mighty kick he shoved open the door, which had been left standing ajar, and strode into the big hall. To Honor it seemed there were a million people there.

"Just what are you all doing here on my honeymoon?" There was no welcome in James's voice, just righteous indignation. He set Honor on her feet, but kept a supporting arm around her. Did he know she would have fallen if he had just put her down?

An indolent figure detached itself from the group. "We came to wish the bride and groom all happiness," said Phillip, smiling as only he could smile. For one instant Honor fought the pain of what might have been, only to have it replaced with relief when he lifted high the glass he was holding.

"Get that booze out of here!" Honor wasn't prepared for James's roar. "You know I don't allow it in this house."

"What's all the shouting about, James?" Babs had crossed to them. "It's just a little drink. We brought our own." The emerald on her finger winked wickedly.

"You're welcome to visit for a little while, but you can't bring that stuff in here."

For one long moment brother faced brother. Honor would never forget it. Seen against the clear and clean-cut features of James, Phillip was a rather smudged carbon copy. Her heart suddenly knew the truth of her words to Carlotta. She had fallen for the strength in Phillip that belonged to his twin. No wonder she had been so relieved to find him different at his ranch than when with the crowd. It was a good thing they paid no attention to her. Would her face give it away?

I must never let James know. He wouldn't, couldn't say he had fallen in love with me. He must never know how right he was. But determination was born. She would make him love her until he was glad he had married her — not to protect her from Phillip, but because he loved her. Hot color spurted into her face, leaving her breathless.

Honor's attention returned to the brothers. Phillip's eyes fell first. "Oh, all right." He carelessly set his drink down, followed by the others. To create a diversion, Honor deliberately stepped forward. "Hello, Phillip." Her quiet voice turned all eyes toward her, slim, smiling, more beautiful in her white gown than they had seen her. Desire rose in Phillip's face, but this time Honor was prepared. She had seen his falseness. Scales had dropped from her vision. "I'm sorry you weren't able to attend our wedding." Suddenly she knew it was true. She was free forever of Phillip Travis.

Phillip couldn't seem to answer. It was red-haired Babs who mocked, "Some little trick, Miss Honor Brooks. So Phillip wasn't here when you arrived? He had — other things on his mind."

"It didn't matter. James welcomed me."

Babs drew in a sharp breath. "I'll say he did! You pulled a real trick in getting old James to the altar. I wonder what Lucille's going to say?" Yet behind her baiting Honor sensed genuine relief in Babs's face, an almost-approval of what had happened. Did she care for Phillip that much?

James broke the uncomfortable silence. "Now if you really must go, I believe Mrs. Travis would like to change."

"The old here's your hat, what's your hurry routine," Babs mocked. "Come on, Phillip. We aren't wanted — or needed here." But the glance she threw over her shoulder at Honor was one of gratitude. "You'll just have to put up with me since your lady love prefers your twin." Over Phillip's protests she dragged him away, but not before he called back, "I'll be home soon."

Honor sighed with relief as the heavy door closed behind them. Slowly she turned to find James watching.

"You did very well, my dear." He stepped nearer, and her heart pounded. Surely he could hear it! She wouldn't have expected his next comment. "How would you like to go for a short ride?"

Honor stared at him, then said, "Why, I'd like that. Let me get changed." She ran up the stairs thinking to herself, *When I get to bed tonight I'll probably cry or scream. Now all I do is go riding with a husband who married me to protect me!*

By the time she had changed, James had Sol and Jingles ready. Silently he helped her mount. She laughed a little at her awkwardness. "I'll be a tenderfoot for some time, I'm afraid."

"Then you'll stay?" Was that restrained eagerness in his voice or her own wishful thinking?

"For a time. It seems a shame to miss out

on a real ranch vacation just because of something so trivial as a mistaken identity wedding." Before he could answer she had prodded Jingles with her heels and was racing down the road.

"Honor, wait!"

What imp of perversity caused her to dig in her heels more? "Come on, Jingles, let's go!" Ignoring the pounding of Sol behind them, she urged her pony forward. Faster, faster, until — Jingles stumbled, went down. Honor felt herself sailing through the air, then blackness enveloped her. A sharp pain stabbed her right shoulder. She cried out and knew nothing more until she lifted heavy lids to find herself cradled in James's arms. She tried to struggle, but the pain in her shoulder was too much.

"Lie still." She felt the swing of a horse. James must have taken her on Sol.

"Jingles threw me. He must have stepped in a hole." She incoherently tried to explain.

"That's why I called. You don't run horses at night or in half-light." His voice was cold and hard. "Jingles hurt his leg pretty bad. I may have to shoot him."

Honor twisted until she could look in his face. "Oh, no!"

Pain crossed the features above her, still visible in the ruby sunset. "I'll call the vet. If it's only sprained, we can use hot compresses to get the swelling down. If it's broken —"

"It's my fault!" The first tears of the whole amazing day slipped from beneath her tightly closed lids. "If you have to shoot Jingles, it's my fault."

He didn't soften the blow. "Yes, it is. If you won't listen to people who know more about ranching than you do, maybe you'd better just stay in the house. Casa del Sol is a beautiful place. It is also a dangerous place. There are wild animals. There are rattlesnakes in the rocks."

Honor shivered, feeling small. "I'm sorry."

He slid to his feet, still carrying her, leaving Sol with reins dragging. "I'll get you in the house and call the vet."

"Senora!" Even through her remorse and pain Honor caught the change in Rosa's greeting. She was Senora now, mistress of Casa del Sol.

"Mrs. Travis has had a bad fall. I'm taking her to her room, Mama Rosa. Bring liniment. Her shoulder is sprained." For all the feeling in James's voice she might have been of less importance than the barn, Honor thought fleetingly. Mama Rosa and Carlotta worked with swift fingers, un-

127

dressing her, getting her shoulder bathed, and dressed with a stinging liniment.

"You will feel better tomorrow. What a way to start a honeymoon!" Carlotta grinned impishly before slipping out the big door, leaving it slightly ajar.

Honeymoon! Honor tried to sit up and failed. She was just too tired to move, physically and emotionally. She threw herself back on the pillow, heedless of the pain in her shoulder. Had she ever lived through such a day? Her wedding day, the day she had dreamed of since she was a child, and especially since she met Phillip. What a travesty! Slow tears seeped into her puffy pillow. It might as well have been a rock. She could no longer put off facing what she had done.

Through her pain and misery came Granny's stern, sad voice, "I don't know what it's going to take to make you see you can't outrun God. When you do, if you are married to an unbeliever, your life will be misery."

A final spurt of rebelliousness brought a protest to her lips, but it died before she could even whisper. No. She couldn't blame God any longer. She had insisted on idolizing Phillip Travis even against her own nagging doubts and the repeated warnings she had been given.

The dimly lit room receded to be replaced first by the scene at the canyon, then later here at Casa del Sol; that momentary, on-the-brink warning. It was not the chill evening breeze from her partly opened window that turned Honor cold. It was memory of her response to God's pleadings — and she knew they had been just that. Instead of listening to the Scriptures that had been planted in her brain, she had been swayed by the beauty of the canyon, the thrill of Phillip's attention, the false assurance that all would be well.

Tossing from one side of the great bed to the other, she faced it head-on. God had not done this to her. She had brought it on herself because she refused to listen to God's call. A new, sharper thrust filled her heart. She struggled to pray, to ask forgiveness, help, peace. *My spirit will not always strive with men* — she remembered the words from Genesis. Why did her prayers only ascend to the ceiling? Was she repenting more for the way things had turned out than for being a sinner? Was she really better off married to a man who obviously despised her than to Phillip? And was what she thought love for James really only clutching for security, strength, someone to stand between her and a world grown harsh?

Her weary brain refused to answer. James must have dropped a sleeping powder in the warm milk he had brought. Even if she could find God and be forgiven for a life of rebellion, she would still have the consequences of her mutiny — either a broken marriage relationship or an unbelieving husband.

7

James Travis kept his promise. In the month following their wedding, Honor saw little of him. Evidently he had meant just what he said. There was no time for leisure. He had a huge ranch to run and did just that.

Honor found she was a special guest as James had promised, nothing more. When he was in for meals, he was quietly courteous, asking if she was enjoying learning to know the ranch. Most of the time he was gone.

Once she curiously asked, "Do you stay in what Mama Rosa calls 'line shacks' when you are out on the range?"

His smile was sardonic, leaving her feeling she had blundered again. "Sometimes. I can't very well stay in the bunkhouse when the hands think this is still our honeymoon."

His thrust had gone home and silenced her.

To Honor, who had been busy all her life, that month was dreamlike. At first it was enough just to rest and sort things out. Yet that very sorting out left her more confused and miserable than ever. It had been as she feared. God's forgiveness would not extend to making everything rosy between James and her. Would they ever be anything except courteous strangers? Neither did she feel God had forgiven her.

She grew thin, worried. In spite of the time she spent with Rosa learning to prepare the spicy Mexican dishes, there wasn't enough to keep her busy. James had forbidden her to ride alone. Sometimes in the evening he took her out, always a stern shadow, an impeccable escort, and as remote as Kendrick Peak.

James unexpectedly appeared at lunch one day. "Would you like to take a drive this afternoon?"

She hid her surprise. "Why, yes. Can you spare the time?" She hadn't meant to sound sarcastic, but it came out that way.

James's expression changed. "I believe it can be arranged."

Nothing more was said until they were seated in the Willys. Honor nervously adjusted a veil. The snowline on the mountains was steadily encroaching upon the valley. No wonder! It was definitely fall. Every leaf flaunted red or gold winter dress in a King Midas world.

"Where are we going?"

"Do you have to ask a question as if I were

still an ogre?" James sounded irritated.

"Aren't you?" Instantly repentant, she laid one gloved hand over his strong one on the wheel, her most unselfconscious gesture since their marriage.

"Don't touch me while I'm driving!"

She snatched her hand back as if it had been burned, more hurt than she would admit even to herself, and made herself small against the door on the passenger side, turning her back on James so he could not read her expression.

"We're going to see an old friend of mine. His name is Judge Bell. I call him Daddy, and have since my own father died."

Something in his voice reached even through Honor's misery. "You really care about him, don't you?"

"I love him and his wife. They're real people."

Honor sneaked a glance at the forbidding face behind the wheel. A ghost of a smile had replaced some of the irritation.

"Judge Bell grew up knowing he was going to be a minister. When he got in his teens he was mixed up in some kind of un-pleasantness — he never said what. He was innocent, but since his comrades were guilty, it looked as if he would be sentenced along with them. The judge in the case was known to be harsh. He was always fair, but the boys knew there was little hope.

"Evidently the judge listened and was impressed by the boy's sincerity. He dismissed the charges against Daddy. Daddy was so impressed he prayed about it, he said, and decided he could do as much good as a Christian judge as if he became a minister. He did. He spent over fifty years as a judge before be retired. Now his heart isn't strong enough for the grueling hours required in his former work."

"What does he do now?"

James laughed. "If you have a picture of a broken down man, you're in for a shock. He ministers. He gives love and comfort to the poor, the dying, even to —" He broke off suddenly, giving her a piercing glance that brought red to her face.

"And you think he can bring comfort to me?"

"I hope so." James swung the big touring car into a small lane. "Honor, I want to talk to you."

Why should his simple statement send shudders up her spine?

"I know you aren't happy. I can't expect you to be, I suppose. Daddy said I did a terrible thing, marrying you as I did."

"He knows?"

"Of course." James's mouth twisted. "I rode over the night after we were married and told him." Bitterness filled his face. "So you don't have to play any games with him. He can see right through you."

I hope not.

Had she spoken the words aloud?

No, James went on uninterrupted. "You'll like him and his wife. They live what they believe." He shot her another quick glance. "By the way, what does that God you believe in — or do you — think about our marriage?"

She chose to answer his first question first. "Yes, I believe in God. I always have. I just never did anything about it — until now." Her voice trailed off.

"Are you a Christian?"

"No." She swallowed a lump in her throat, feeling constricted almost to the point of being unable to breathe. "But I want to be, James, I want to be!" Forgetting the estrangement between them, she turned to face him directly. "From the time I was small I blamed God for everything that went wrong. Granny tried to tell me everyone who lives on earth is subject to natural consequences, but I wouldn't listen." Her troubled face reflected her struggles. "I'm afraid I waited and rebelled too long."

"Ridiculous! What have you ever done that was so terrible? You haven't killed or anything like that. You have lived a good life."

Honor shook her head. "I've sinned most of all by refusing to listen to the Holy Spirit sent to show me what God wants — and by turning my back on the gift of eternal life and salvation through acceptance of God's only Son." She turned away, eyes desolate.

James cleared his throat. "I can't help you with that, but Judge Bell can." He changed the subject. "You didn't tell me what your God thought of our marriage." His lips curved downward. "You think God punished you for not accepting Him by letting you marry an ogre?"

"I can't blame God for what I insisted on." Her lips quivered.

With a muttered imprecation James started the car and drove in silence to a small white cottage with a picket fence, leaving Honor to stare at the blurring countryside they passed.

If ever there was a case of love at first sight it was between Honor and the Bells. "Why, you remind me of my father!" Honor's spontaneous remark was met with warmth like flames of an open fire.

"Come in, come in, children." Motherly

Mrs. Bell and the equally welcoming judge threw wide the door, but after only a few moments the Judge said, "Run along, James. I'll be wanting to talk with your lassie alone."

"Well!" Mrs. Bell's crinkling eyes belied her pretended hurt. "We've been dismissed, James, my boy. We'll go get our doughnuts ready for when they've finished."

Honor waited for Judge Bell to speak. When he did it was to ask her to call him Daddy.

"You know what happened?" She couldn't hide her trembling fingers.

"Aye. But I wonder if you do?"

It was the last thing Honor had expected. "Wh-what do you mean?"

"Did the laddie tell you why?"

A shake of the head was all she could manage.

"I thought not." The soft burr in Daddy Bell's Scottish voice soothed her as nothing had done for weeks. She leaned forward.

"Did — did he tell *you* why?"

"He told me more than he realized. After you had mistaken him for Phillip and went upstairs he paced his library for hours. He ran the gamut of emotions from wanting to horsewhip Phillip to wishing he had never been born twin to such a philanderer.

"He had tried to send you away. He had tried to warn you what Phillip was and you refused to believe. If he told you he was Phillip's brother, you would have more reason to distrust him."

Honor flushed, remembering how she had referred to the absent brother as the ogre.

"Early in life James and Phillip's father had given James charge over his brother, a brother's-keeper responsibility. When Phillip refused direction, James became bitter. When you appeared, it was the last bit of evidence of Phillip's nature to convict him.

"James could see you would never break your vow. He decided to marry you. It had taken an entire night to decide, and he could no longer stand the confines of the library. He saddled Sol, rode here, and caught me just as I was coming in from a call. He —"

Honor could stand no more. Her eyes flew open. "He *told* you what he was going to do?"

"Of course not. Much as I love the laddie, he knew I'd not stand by for such a thing."

The crisp tone brought a wave of color to Honor's face. "I'm sorry. It's just that it's all been such a shock."

"I understand. Lassie," — Daddy Bell's eyes were kind — "did you not know down in your heart Phillip Travis was no man for you?"

It was the final touch. Honor put her face in her hands. "I knew. God even tried to warn me."

A light came to the old man's eyes. "You are a follower?"

"Any following I've done is after my own way."

"And now you're sorry."

"With all my heart." Honor slipped to the hand-braided rug at his feet. "Not just for choosing Phillip over God, but for everything. For not listening to Granny and my brother and —" her voice dropped until it was barely audible "— and the Holy Spirit."

She heard grave concern in his voice as he asked, "Lassie, did you not know the Spirit's calling?"

"That's what is so terrible. I deliberately chose Phillip Travis over God!" She scarcely heard his quick intake of breath. "Now when I try to pray, it's as if God has turned His back on me — just as I did on Him."

"Look at me."

There was something magnificent in Daddy Bell's voice reminiscent of days when he tempered justice with mercy. Honor fixed her gaze on his face.

"Do you recognize now how much of a sinner you are? Do you freely acknowledge it, and believe Jesus died to save you from those sins? Do you accept Him into your heart and life forever?"

"Yes!"

The soft cry in the still room seemed magnified in Honor's ears. Daddy Bell's admonition, "Tell Him so," brought a rush of feeling as Honor stammered, "I'm a sinner, God. Forgive me. I accept the gift of your Son and salvation through Him." She could not go on. The month of sleepless nights had taken their toil, but the next instant she felt weariness leave. In its place was peace — not the false assurance that she could work things out, but the knowledge that no matter what came, God was there to strengthen her. Along with the peace was knowledge — she was free, forgiven. But it did not mean every trouble was over. She was just what Granny had said she would be — wedded to one who scorned the Christ, or at best ignored Him, just as she had done.

Another memory found its way to her lips. "I said, when Granny warned me, that if God ever caught up to me, there was no reason He couldn't catch Phillip, too." Her regret struck deep. "How blind, willful, sinful I was!"

Daddy Bell's hands were warm on her own. "It's over, lassie. I won't try and excuse you in any way for what you have done. You must live with it. Neither will I excuse James." His shrewd eyes searched her. "I will say I doubt the laddie married you entirely to save you from Phillip."

"He despises me as a weakling." Honor couldn't hold back tears. "How can you say he might care?"

"It has been my business to know men."

Daddy Bell's words echoed in Honor's mind as James and Mrs. Bell came in, to be told the news of Honor's acceptance of Christ. Mrs. Bell appeared delighted. James did not. On the way home he spoke of it. "I suppose now you're a Christian you'll be even more bitter about me." He didn't give her a chance to reply, but quickly added, "What does God say about Christian wives with husbands like me?"

She sought sarcasm and found none. Was he serious? She would respond as if he was. "First Corinthians seven fourteen says, 'For the unbelieving husband is sanctified by the wife, and —' "

"The Bible doesn't say that!" James shot her a glance that was totally unreadable.

"See for yourself. It's right there."

"If I had a Bible, I might just do that."

Honor rode quietly all the way home. When they reached the sprawling hacienda she climbed from the car without waiting for his assistance, only saying, "Thank you for taking me." She dashed upstairs, threw open the big trunk she had brought from San Francisco, and delved clear to the bottom. For a moment she held close the precious Book she unearthed. She would need it now more than ever. As a child of God, she must study.

With a sigh she touched the worn cover regretfully, then lifted her chin. Daddy Bell would get her another Bible. In the meantime —

James looked shocked when she appeared, out of breath at the bottom of the stairs. "What on earth —"

"Here." She steadied her voice, forcing casualness into it she did not feel. "I have been wondering what to give you — whether to give you this —" She held it out.

"A Bible?"

The trancelike state he seemed to have gone into released a spirit she hadn't known existed. "It's perfectly proper to accept, Mr. Travis. Even it we weren't married, a Bible is always considered an acceptable gift."

She retreated up two steps, away from the disturbing dark eyes. "Don't forget to read it — especially First Corinthians." Her sense of mischief faded. "And John, especially three sixteen —" She couldn't go on, so blindly ran upstairs, remembering how he stood staring at her. She gently closed her door and dropped to her knees by the side of the bed. How easy it was to tell someone else to read the best-known of all verses, "For God so loved the world, that he gave his only begotten Son, that whosoever believeth in him should not perish, but have everlasting life." But how hard it had been to accept it!

Tears drenched the beautiful spread. If only she had accepted that verse and invited Jesus into her heart, asking for forgiveness for her sins long ago when Keith did, how different things would be now! She would not be in love with a husband who cared nothing for her and even less for the Lord she had suddenly discovered was more precious to her than anything else on earth.

8

That was only the first of Honor's visits to the Bell cottage. James took time from his duties on the ranch to teach Honor to drive, and once she was competent, she traveled to the little home near Kendrick Peak often. Each visit produced growth in her Christian walk.

One particularly beautiful afternoon she said, "Daddy, all the Scriptures I have known practically forever mean something now. Is it because I am reading with my heart?"

"Aye, lassie." The wise eyes lit with an inner glow. "Faith is the key to unlock the mysteries of the universe."

Inevitably their talks included James. Daddy was firm in the belief James would come to know God as other than a Master Mind. "He's a pantheist, you know." He intercepted Honor's questioning glance. "One who equates God with nature and the laws of the universe."

"Is it wrong to see God in nature? At the canyon I felt something of this." Honor's face was wistful, remembering the beauty and magnificence of the place.

"There is nothing wrong with seeing God as Creator of this earth's glory so long as you don't lose sight of God — the Father, the Son, and the Holy Spirit, who brought salvation to this world."

"And James only sees the creating force." A shadow crossed her face. "Daddy, who is Lucille Lawson?"

The old man looked surprised at the change of subject. "Why, she's a twice-divorced woman who —" he looked a bit shamefaced, and Honor could see him carefully choosing words "— who had designs on James and his ranch." He peered at her more closely. "How did you hear of her?"

"Her name was mentioned by Babs and the crowd the day I was married. I also saw it on an envelope in the library."

"She's not your kind — or James's."

Honor spread her hands wide. "Who is?" Her honest eyes met Daddy's. "He is such a mass of contradictions. Laughing one moment, locked behind a granite wall the next. I know he doesn't drink or go in for that sort of thing." Her face shadowed. "Because of my stubbornness here I am married to him. I'm learning the terrible results of sin. If I hadn't insisted on my own way, James would be free."

"Are you sure he wants to be?" The quiet voice cut through her depression.

"How can he help it? He laughed when he

told me how he even arranged with Juan to come dashing out with the telegram supposedly telling Phillip was coming. It did say that, but James had already known Phillip was due soon." She stopped, trouble chasing away the joy that always came through her learning sessions with Daddy. "Such a quixotic gesture! He seems honorable enough, except for that —"

"Would you have thought of yourself as honorable before meeting Phillip Travis?"

"I would have then."

"Yet you chose not only to marry Phillip but to deny every teaching you have been given," Daddy gently reminded. "I cannot say why James did such a thing. When he came to me after the wedding and told me, I was stunned. I cried out in protest, asked how he could deliberately plot and arrange this marriage."

Honor held her breath in the little pause that followed.

The judge's face was stern. "He told me that even though you persisted in believing nothing but the best of Phillip, he couldn't stand to see you crushed under his brother's boots like a frail flower."

"I really thought Phillip would change, especially after coming to Casa del Sol."

She couldn't believe the way Daddy's big

hand balled into a fist and struck the shining edge of a piecrust table. "Lassie, any girl or woman who marries a man in hopes of reforming him is doomed to a living hell on earth! If it is not in a man to live clean and honorably before marriage, only rarely will he do it after."

"Yet you refuse to see my marriage to James as a tragedy." Honor regretted the words as soon as they came out.

Daddy Bell's face settled into deep lines. "I would have given anything on earth to prevent it. Now it is done, you can only go on from here."

"I know." She stood and restlessly walked toward the window. "Even when I was being married I sensed something wrong. I refused to admit how weak Phillip was. He needed me. Since accepting Christ I have begun to see the awfulness of what God saved me from, and it is from my own actions."

"It always is."

Honor turned back toward him. "It's just that I don't know how to approach him. I don't know if he reads the Bible I gave him. Even if he does, he never mentions it."

"You've stayed in spite of everything. Are you going to continue to honor your vows?"

147

Honor looked deep into the searching eyes. "I must. I promised before God and man, gave my word." She bit her lips to steady them. "Unless he sends me away."

"And do you want to stay, lassie?" Before she could answer, his face crimsoned. "Forgive me." He held out both hands to Honor. "I have no right to ask such a thing."

He deliberately changed the subject. "The only good whatsoever I can see coming from such a beginning lies in your heart, and in the life James has led since childhood. He hates anything smacking of cheapness."

Honor nodded, and Daddy continued, "He also believes in God but has not yet met Him, face to face. He cannot admit he is a sinner and claim forgiveness through Jesus' death on Calvary."

"Will he ever?"

"He must!" Daddy dropped her hands to bring his fist down against the arm of the chair. "He knows the way. But it may take a long, hard road of traveling before James Travis accepts the gift of salvation through our Lord Jesus."

"Just as it was a long, hard road for me."

Daddy sighed. "Yes. I cannot condone in any way what the two of you have done. Neither is there any time for crying over the past. You must go forward and leave what will be in God's hands."

"You will pray for us?" It was through a blur that Honor saw his benedictory smile.

"I have been — since James came with the news. Live your faith so he can see it is real. Your refusing to break your vows will be a witness."

Mrs. Bell's round, smiling face appeared in the doorway. "Honor, one of these days I'll teach you to make some of my special recipes. James loves them." In the general conversation following, Honor's depression could not help vanishing. She laughed. "It will be a real accomplishment when I can equal your doughnuts!"

"Anything worth knowing is worth working at," Daddy reminded, leaving Honor with a parting word. She knew it was not to doughnuts, but to her own life and walk with God that he referred.

Several days later she told Rosa, "It's good to be back in the kitchen." Her floury hands stilled on the big board where she was practicing making tortillas. "I haven't had a chance since Granny died, and I'm really a homemaker at heart."

"It is good. Senor's woman should be home, not off working for others." Rosa snorted. "Flagstaff women are leaving homes and children. Pah! They should stay home where they belong."

Honor hid a smile. What would Rosa, happy with her pots and pans, think of San Francisco, where women were flocking to offices! "Where do the cowhands eat?" she asked.

"The cookhouse." Rosa's white smile widened. "I show you when everyone is gone. Cookie likes my pies, but no visitors."

It took weeks for Honor to discover how big her new home really was. James began to take her around more, as if she were a special guest. She could almost forget their unusual marriage at the sight of the birds, coyotes, a startled deer.

"Honor," he asked on one of the expeditions, "are you unhappy here?"

"No." Before he could reply, she remounted the pony who had replaced Jingles. Although her favorite pinto would recover, he wasn't to be ridden for a time. When she was in the saddle she looked down. "When I forget about — about that ceremony, I am not unhappy."

"I'm glad." He covered her rapidly tanning hands with his own. Something in the dark eyes flickered, making her wonder if Daddy Bell could be right. Was her husband beginning to care for her? It was the first time he had touched her since their wedding day.

Breathless, unwilling to acknowledge what she either saw or imagined, Honor touched her horse with her heels. "Race you back to the ranch!" The spell was broken. She felt the wind in her face and, exulting, cried out encouragement to her pony. She felt rather than saw when James caught up with her. The longer stride of Sol easily overtook her pony.

"Faster, faster," she urged, but always he was there beside them, laughing above the wind she created with her momentum. Neck and neck they raced to the corral. At the last moment Sol leaped ahead and left Honor and her mount to come in second.

"You could at least have let me win," she complained as she slid from the saddle, refusing his help. "Seems it would be the polite thing to do!" Her disheveled hair surrounded the hat that had slid back until it was only held by the cord around her throat. Strangely stirred inside, she felt the need to pick a quarrel of some kind to relieve the tension, even if it was only over a silly race.

"Is that what you want — to be let to win?"

If the quizzical question had a hidden meaning, she chose to ignore it. Stepping close, hands on hips in an easy Western pose, she glared at him. "I intend to beat you fair and square, Mr. Man. And I'll do it with honor."

Her pretended indignation slipped at what she saw in his face. The combination of tenderness and kindness almost proved her undoing. Quickly she turned back to her horse. "I'm going to begin by showing you how well I can unsaddle my horse and rub him down." Her deft hands that had practiced hours in secret for this very moment made short work of lifting the heavy saddle. She staggered a bit, but triumphantly got it where it belonged and went on to groom down her horse in the best way possible.

"Say, you're going to make a pretty good rancher's wife after all!" He took one step toward her, a new admiration showing.

Honor's heart flipped over. The intensity of her own emotion almost overwhelmed her, but the feeling was interrupted.

"Really, darling, it takes more than being able to rub down a horse to be wife of the heir of Casa del Sol!"

Honor whirled toward the speaker. Soignee, every shining blonde hair in place, green eyes smiling maliciously, the woman was everything Honor was not at that moment! Acutely aware of her own appearance, Honor flushed deeply. Who was this woman?

"Hello, Lucille." James's voice was flat, unemotional.

So this is Lucille! Honor boiled as the woman tucked her hand in James's arm and smiled up into his face. "I understand congratulations are in order. This must be the little bride?" She lifted highly painted lips and kissed James square on the mouth. Honor had the satisfaction of seeing him recoil.

"Always dramatic, aren't you, Lucille? What brings you out here?"

"Curiosity." The boldness of her statement left Honor speechless. "I ran into Phillip. He told me he was carefully staying away from the ranch for a while — until the honeymoon was over."

So that was why Phillip hadn't come as promised. Honor's mind ran double track, wondering why Lucille had come.

"Mrs. Lawson is an old friend," James explained. "Lucille, my wife, Honor."

"Honor!" The heavily-made-up eyes widened. "How quaint!"

It was too much. Honor's good nature had been strained. "Yes, isn't it? But then, I'm a bit quaint myself. Perhaps that is why James married me." She saw his jaw drop, and smiled sweetly at their guest. "I must excuse myself and tell Mama Rosa there will be a guest for dinner. You will stay, won't you?"

"I'll stay." With the tables turned, Lucille sounded grim.

"Then I'll see you later."

"Do you dress for dinner?"

Honor thought rapidly, then disarmingly touched her rumpled clothing. "Doesn't it look like we need to dress for dinner?" She walked steadily toward the house before Lucille could answer. This was one time she felt she needed to dress for dinner. The horrible truth dawned on her — she had no evening gown except the white dress she had been married in!

Giggling nervously at the hastily contrived trap that had caught her, she burst into the house. "Mama Rosa! Come quick!"

"Senora, what is it?" An alarmed brown face peered from the doorway, closely followed by Carlotta's anxious one.

"A Mrs. Lawson has arrived —"

"Her!" Carlotta's sniff was a masterpiece. "Mrs. La-De-Dah in person!"

"Exactly." Honor felt herself relaxing under their understanding. "She was hateful, wondered about dressing for dinner. I told her yes. But I don't have anything except my wedding gown!"

"Wear it," Carlotta advised. "Wait!" She dashed into the open courtyard and returned triumphantly with a handful of late roses. "Mama can put up your hair and tuck a flower in it." Her skillful fingers were twining the flowers even as she spoke, carefully removing thorns, fashioning a beautiful corsage. "This goes on your left shoulder."

When Honor was dressed, her two faithful friends stepped back in admiration. "Beautiful!" Carlotta clapped her hands, but Mama Rosa only smiled and said, "Senor will be proud."

He was. Honor could see it in his eyes when she descended the curving staircase. Lucille Lawson stood close, shivering in a backless ice-green gown.

"Why, Mrs. Lawson, come in where it's warm! That hall of ours does stay cold." Honor threw open the door to the library. "James, why did you leave her standing out there?" She didn't wait for an answer. "Tell me, are you here for long?"

Slightly disconcerted, but unwilling to allow anyone else to steal the stage for even a minute, the green eyes matching her gown hardened. "I really don't know. That is, when I came back to Phoenix — I've been shopping in New Yawk, you know — well, I just heard about the wedding and rushed right out here with a gift." She handed a heavy box to Honor.

For one moment Honor felt like throwing it into the fireplace, then her own breeding replaced the urge with a quiet smile. "It was kind of you to think of us. James, will you open it, or shall I?"

"Go ahead." If the tone of his voice was an indication, they were in for cold weather during Mrs. Lawson's stay.

Honor hesitated, noting the expensive label on the box. She wanted nothing from this woman, especially her gifts. Why had she come, just when things might have improved with James? Keeping her face bland she lifted the contents of the package. "Oh!" She dropped it back in its wrappings, unable to conceal her distaste. James came to her rescue, holding up the platter surrounded with heavily carved silver snakes.

"Lucille, that has to be the ugliest thing I have ever seen."

"Why, Jimmy!" She pouted. "It's solid silver. I thought you'd like it — to remember me by."

His voice was grimmer than Honor had ever heard it. "Then if it's solid silver I'm afraid we'll have to say thank you and return it. We couldn't possibly accept a present so valuable. *Or inappropriate,*" he muttered just loud enough for Honor to catch.

"Sorry, darling." Steel blades unsheathed themselves in her green eyes. "Just thought I'd bring you a reminder of all our past — associations."

"What is that supposed to mean?" James Travis caught her by the shoulders, swinging her around to face him. "You know there's never been anything between us."

"Oh?" She pointed a woman-to-woman glance at Honor, who stood frozen in place. "Of course, darling, if you say so."

"I do say so. To be brutally frank, you've been a nightmare. There hasn't been a time you haven't followed me and tried to give the impression of some hidden relationship between us."

"Poor boy." She stroked his cheek with a white hand she had managed to free. Honor stood like a statue, wondering. *How can she do it? I would be scared to death if James looked at me like that. There's almost murder in his eyes!*

"Don't touch me!" James loosened her so she nearly fell. He jerked the bell rope nearby. Honor could hear it pealing in the distance. Time stood suspended until Juan appeared, almost running. "Senor?"

"Mrs. Lawson won't be staying for dinner. Please show her out, Juan."

Honor gasped as Lucille Lawson went a dull, murderous red. It was her turn to shoot hateful sparks into the air. "So, it's true! This baby-faced little thing has you snared. You think she'll ever have brains enough to be mistress of Casa del Sol? The way I hear it, she fell in Phillip's arms like am overripe apple, got herself invited down here." She spun back to Honor. "What happened? Did you find bigger game?"

"That's enough!" James seized her by the arm and propelled her to the door, only stopping to scoop up the offending silver gift. The eyes of the carved snakes glittered in the dim light. "Get out and take your snakes with you!"

Honor heard their footsteps across the tiled floor of the hall then the dull thud as the heavy door banged into place. She dropped in a chair, exhausted by the scene, frantically searching for something to say when James returned.

He came back, breathing hard. Without a word he crossed to the fireplace and poked its already blazing contents into a minor inferno.

"Well?" She hadn't known her voice

could be so weak and trembly.

"Well, what?" The anger in his eyes was directed at her now.

"Well, Mrs. Lawson — she —" Honor was unable to go on.

"She's a troublemaker and always has been."

Honor waited, but he didn't go on. How could he so casually dismiss that vicious woman? Gnawing doubt crept into her heart. "She must have had something to base all that on. It's hard to imagine any woman bursting into a honeymoon —" She turned fiery, but forced herself to continue. "Unless she had been given some kind of reason to expect —"

James towered over her, tall, terrible, as she had seen him earlier. "She has never been given any reason to expect anything!" Honor's sigh of relief was lost in his fury. "The only mistake I ever made was in treating her as a human being and not telling her to get lost every time she hung around." He laughed bitterly. "You're my wife. In spite of everything I shouldn't have had to tell you that. Do you believe me?"

She was so startled by his abrupt question she could only stammer, "I — I —"

His laugh was even more bitter. "It

doesn't really matter. Think what you like. I don't care either way."

"Then since you don't care, I won't bother to answer." Honor rose, her heart dropping like lead. He didn't care, at all. She managed a dignified exit until she got just to the doorway of the library. "Why did she have to come? This afternoon I thought maybe we could be friends —" Her words died on her lips.

"Friends?" James looked at her as if she had dropped in from outer space. "I'm afraid not. Friends are people who trust you." He brushed past her, arrogantly striding toward the door. "I don't believe I care for any dinner. I'm going out on Sol."

Again she heard footsteps cross the tile floor, the same thud of the big door closing. This time she did not try to think of something to say. She was seething with fury.

"You come to dinner now?" Mama Rosa peered into the library. "Juan say Mrs. Lawson is gone. But where is Senor?"

The innocent question brought even more fury to Honor. "I don't know and don't care. I don't want any dinner." She ran for the staircase, trailing the white dress she had put on so eagerly such a short time before. "Senor can go where he pleases. I don't care what he does!" Passing Mama with her shocked face, Honor pelted up the stairs, bolted her door, and fell on the bed.

"Let him go! Let him go riding. I don't care if he never comes back. Why should he take it out on me? Just because I couldn't instantly say I had full trust in him! How could he expect me to trust him, after what he pulled about our wedding?" The next instant she was on her knees, crying her heart out. "Oh, God, what am I going to do?"

Hours later she heard Sol's rhythmic gait. She had learned to distinguish it from that of the other horses. Carefully she slipped to the window, watching as she had watched other times. Even from this distance she could see James's restrained fury. Angry with her? Or Lucille? Or both? Did he regret the mad impulse that had caused him to marry her in a quixotic plan to save her from his brother?

Cold air struck her the same time fear hit. Perhaps now he would realize how insane it had all been and send her away. The new thought paralyzed her and sent her shivering back to the big bed. Wave after wave of fear went through her. He would send her away. She would never see him again. Too numb to pray, still her heart pleaded, "No, don't let it happen! I love him." But only the cold night wind answered by its frosty breath. Half-frozen, she finally stumbled from bed and closed the window. No use trying to sleep. She touched a match to the always-laid fire in her tiny fireplace and cuddled in front of it wrapped in a robe and the comforter from the bed. Gradually the little fire warmed her.

As the heaviest frost of the season turned every branch and twig into a carrier of white rime that sparkled in the first rays of dawn, she wrestled with her problem. Body warm, heart still a chunk of ice, she at last slipped into bed, too worn out to think any more.

The next day Phillip Travis came home.

9

" 'Home is the sailor, home from the sea,' and all that." Phillip Travis's debonair manner disappeared as he slumped into a chair. Honor had been trying to read in the library without much success. Every footstep on the tiled hall floor brought her heart to her throat. She expected James to come in, look at her coldly, and order her to go.

Her relief was so great that she welcomed Phillip more warmly than she would have thought possible. "Hello! We've been wondering when you would come."

"Oh?" The dark eyes were wary. "Wouldn't have thought you'd care one way or the other now that you're all hitched up with James."

Choosing her words carefully, Honor insisted, "We will always care about you, Phillip." Her gentle voice attested to the truth of her words.

"Sure you will. That's why you came down here and married James within a week of the time we were engaged."

"I can explain that —" But Honor stopped short. She couldn't explain. It would be too humiliating.

Phillip didn't seem to notice. He was staring moodily into the roaring fire that was always kept going now that the weather had turned colder. "I might have known. You were always too good for me. It's really better this way." He grinned crookedly at her shocked expression. "I mean it. I'm a rotten guy. James can make you happy."

It was the last thing on earth she would have expected from him. "You — you really mean that."

"Sure." He looked surprised. "Even at the canyon I knew it wouldn't last." He caught her disillusionment and leaned forward. "I'm just no good, Honor. At least not for a girl like you. I even wish I could be, but not all the time."

From somewhere deep inside Honor was given insight, as she had at the canyon. "Phillip, if you have even a desire to change, God will help you if you will only —"

"Don't preach, Honor." But there was no anger in his voice. "Funny, I'm James's twin, and *he* isn't always drunk or gambling." Again there was a note of wistfulness. "But of course, he has the ranch to look after."

"And you? What do you have to look after?"

For one moment she thought she had

probed too deeply, but Phillip only stared at her, then lazily yawned. "Me, I guess." He yawned again. "A long time ago I thought I'd have Babs to look after, but she had other ideas."

Eyes steady, forcing him to look at her, Honor said, "I believe Babs cares for you more than you know."

There was a quick flare of hope in his eyes, replaced by dullness. "Too late. I don't care about her."

"Don't you, Phillip?" Without giving him a chance to answer, Honor stood. "Why don't you invite Babs for a visit? Give her a chance to be something other than your 'good-time' date. You might be surprised."

"At least it would be something different. I'm about fed up with the social whirl. Maybe I will give her a call." He slumped back and closed his eyes, but Honor thoughtfully went to her room. Did she dare? She did. She would dare anything to help that troubled man downstairs. Her original love for him had died, but there was another reason to help him now. He was James's brother, weak, perhaps foolish, but still James's brother — and hers, if she stayed.

Gently she picked up the phone and rang. "Operator? Please give me the number of

Barbara Merrill in Flagstaff." She didn't want to let Phillip see her searching for the number. "Babs, this is Honor Brooks Travis." She could hear unfriendliness and suspicion in the other woman's voice, but rushed on, "I believe Phillip may be going to call and invite you here. You will be welcome. Phillip needs you." There was a long pause, along with the thudding of Honor's heart, then Babs's slightly thawed voice said, "Thanks." Was that a husky note?

Honor cradled the phone. Had James been right when he said Babs was waiting for Phillip to prove he could be true? It was odd, out of keeping with her own sheltered life. Such games and social ploys were out of her sphere. Babs seemed to be sophisticated — was it possible she wanted a lasting marriage? Honor would have judged her as someone to try again if the first time didn't work.

Soberly Honor donned her riding outfit. It didn't pay to judge. But how strange it would be if it turned out Babs was one of the first she would be called to witness to about her recent experience in acceptance of Christ! Her heart sank. What a task! Yet if God gave her the task, He would send strength to do it.

Babs had sounded almost thunderstruck

when she hung up. The next few days might be quite interesting!

When Honor got downstairs, Phillip was waiting. This time his lazy manner failed to hide his eagerness. "I called Babs. She's coming and will be here for dinner." Suddenly he dropped his pose. "I don't blame you for throwing me down after you met James. We can at least be friends, can't we?"

Without her own volition Honor parroted James's words to her from the afternoon before. "Friends are people who trust you."

"I trust you, Honor." Phillip stepped closer, looking up to her on the second stair above him. "I don't know why you married James in such a hurry, but it's all right."

"Oh, Phillip." Blindly she reached out a hand to be caught in the white ones shaped like James's hands but so different in color and texture from the working hands she had learned to love!

"What a touching scene." The sarcasm in James's voice effectively separated the two on the stairs. "Welcoming the prodigal home, Honor? Don't overdo it." He brushed past them rudely. Honor clung to the banister rail in order to keep from being upset.

"Just a minute!"

Honor had never seen such determination in Phillip's eyes. It must have startled

James. He swung around, looking back down with intense dislike in his face.

"Honor was kind enough to suggest that I ask Babs for a visit. I told her Babs was coming and asked Honor to be my friend. That's why she gave me her hand."

"My wife needs no explanation of her actions to me by you or anyone — especially by you." James's face was granite, his eyes flint. "If Babs is coming I would suggest you remember she is your guest. My wife will make her welcome, of course." Had there been the slightest emphasis on the words *my wife?*

Phillip started up the stairs. "Why, you —"

"Phillip, no!" With a horror of scenes, Honor caught his arm. He mustn't fight his own brother on her account! She had longed to bring peace to this house, not contention. "You must not fight! Either of you." She scornfully looked at James. "Phillip told you the truth. If you don't want to believe him, that's your problem."

"Then since it doesn't matter, I won't commit myself. We'll be dressing for dinner, I suppose, in Babs's honor?"

Tears of fury stung Honor's eyes. He had parried her plea for trust as effectively as she had done the day before. "Yes, we will dress for dinner." She turned her back squarely on him. "Phillip, I don't seem to have the proper clothing for Casa del Sol and its visitors. Perhaps you and Babs will drive in with me to Flagstaff one day this week. I'm sure Babs can tell me where to buy."

Only the sneaking admiration in Phillip's eyes held her together. Had she been expected to knuckle under? Perhaps as Phillip had done — too often? With a weaker personality it must have been much easier just to take the line of least resistance.

"I'll give you a check when you want to go shopping."

Resisting an impulse to kick him in the shins or say something even more sarcastic than he had done, Honor counted to ten and turned. She would not lose her belief in a soft answer's turning away wrath simply because this man infuriated and goaded her beyond belief. Her voice was low and even. "That won't be necessary." She even managed a smile. "After all, brides provide their own trousseaus."

She thought he would protest. His face had thunderclouded to a scowl. At the last moment he changed tactics, stepping aside and sweeping her a low bow. "As you say, my dear." For the first time since the wedding he turned and caught her to him, kissing her lightly on the forehead. "Sorry I was cross. Why don't you have a ride before dinner? There's plenty of time." As if forgetting why he had been going upstairs, James trod heavily down and across the hall, leaving the door ajar behind him.

Phillip smiled. "You've got him befuddled, Honor. He wants to believe in you but isn't too sure about me." He grinned, yet an anxious look crept into his face. "I suppose I should be flattered, but I really don't want to cause trouble between you two. He's the biggest thing in my life. I've always wanted to be more like him."

Honor again caught the cry for help. "There's no reason you can't, Phillip. If you would only believe in yourself — and in God."

"I really can't see myself in that role." He shook his head.

"I can — with all my heart." Her fervent exclamation scored, and a bit awkwardly Phillip asked, "How about that ride? We certainly have James's blessing."

Honor swallowed a lump in her throat. James's change of direction had been superb showmanship, nothing more. The kiss had not held tenderness, as had his kisses before their wedding. It had all been for Phillip's benefit. Dashing back disappointment, she forced gaiety. "Of course!

170

How long has it been since you've really ridden here? I bet I know more about Casa del Sol than you do!"

"We'll see about that!"

But an hour later Phillip had to admit defeat. "You're right. You really do know more. I guess I've been too busy indoors to remember how grand it is." His sweeping hand took in the still-yellow aspens, towering firs and pines, and distance-softened rolling hills leading to mountains dusted by early snow. "You think Babs will like it?"

Honor whirled toward him. "Phillip, I want to know right now — why did you pay all that attention to me — build up promises? You know you've never really loved anyone but Babs!"

She didn't think he would answer, and when he did it was in a shamed voice. "I know. But you were different, sweet. When Babs turned me down I made up my mind I'd never let her hurt me again. She —" He stopped, forced himself to look at Honor. "When I was at the canyon I really did think maybe I could make it with you."

"It was a terrible thing to do, Phillip."

Her gently accusing voice brought color even to his ears. "I know — now. But it all turned out all right. You married James. You could have searched the world over and never found a better man."

"Does your brother know how much you care about him?"

"Don't be ridiculous!" The mood was broken. "Men don't go around telling each other stuff like that."

"You're the one who is ridiculous. He's your brother. If you had let him know a long time ago how you feel, a lot of the trouble between you could have been solved before it began."

"Maybe you're right." But it was too serious for Phillip. "Come on — race you to the ranch!"

"Didn't think you could do it," he teased as he reined in beside her. "A tenderfoot like you beating an old hand like me?"

"An old hand like you had better do more riding. You're getting rusty. Next time I'll beat you worse!" Honor swung from the saddle and prepared to remove it.

"Hey, let one of the hands do that."

"What? A good rancher takes care of his own, or her own, horse. Get that saddle off and your mount rubbed down."

"That's telling him," a soft voice applauded. Babs Merrill leaned against the door laughing at them, even more beautiful than when Honor had seen her before.

"Babs, welcome!" Honor stepped toward

her, a smile lighting her face. "I won't offer to shake hands — they're pretty dirty!"

"That won't stop me." Phillip took the well-groomed hands in his own grimy ones. Honor saw the look in his eyes and turned her back. Who would have thought she wouldn't have minded? She busied herself with her horse, glad for the activity to keep pace with her galloping thoughts. She really didn't mind. She only hoped Phillip could find happiness. Would Babs ever be interested in learning about God? How much happier they could be if they knew Him! She closed her lips tight. She wouldn't preach.

She didn't have to. After the leisurely dinner interspersed with laughter, Babs excused herself and went upstairs. Wondering, Honor followed to see if there was anything needed in the ornate guest suite. Babs's room door was open, but she wasn't there. Strange. Honor glanced in the open door of the guest suite bathroom. No Babs. Her own door stood open. Had Babs gone there?

Babs was sitting on Honor's bed when Honor entered. "Why did you invite me here? Another of your do-gooder deeds?" But her voice held only a flick of her usual sarcasm. "Why did you say Phillip needed me?"

"Because it's true." Honor saw the doubt

mixed with hope in green eyes gone suddenly soft. The long, slender fingers trembled. Honor knew what she must do. "Babs, you were right at the canyon. Phillip saw me as a summer romance."

"And you?"

"Much more." She could be candid, open, without fear of hurt. "I was lonely. I saw everything in Phillip I'd ever wanted. Yet I also knew it would take a miracle for us to ever be happy. I wanted to believe Phillip had a longing inside for something more than his present way of life. I felt I had something to offer him." She fell silent for a moment. "Babs, I still do."

Honor saw Babs stiffen, resentment oozing from every pore.

"Wait! Not what you think, Babs! I'm married to James. I have no love for Phillip at all."

"So you didn't marry James for his money!" Babs had the grace to flush. "Maybe I've misjudged you. You're really in love with him, aren't you?"

Honor was speechless — that this woman of the world could so easily shatter her defenses.

"Honor, forgive me. But what did you mean, you still have something to offer Phillip?"

Honor's tongue was released. "I have the Lord Jesus Christ to offer Phillip. A better friend, a finer companion than anyone on earth could ever be. He's there for the taking."

Babs looked disappointed. "Oh. You mean religion."

"Not exactly." Honor's face glowed with determination. She had been given a chance to witness without preaching. She would do just that. "Religion encompasses many things. But the belief in and acceptance of Jesus Christ as your Savior is much more! God sent His only Son to earth that we might know Him and have eternal life."

"You really believe that? Why?"

Honor thought for a moment. "Babs, I was only a child when my parents were killed in the San Francisco earthquake. But I had my brother, Keith, to look after and Granny to lean on. Then Keith died somewhere in France. Granny followed. I was left alone, so alone I wished I could die, too." Tears glittered but did not fall. "For a time I was numb, uncaring. Then I knew my life had to count for something. Their work was over, mine was not."

"You mean this God of yours took away the pain?" Babs was frankly disbelieving, but at least she was listening.

"No, Babs." Honor faced her guest steadily. "The pain is there, but God has given me extra strength so I can live with it." She was encouraged by Babs's face, the almost reluctant fascination.

"Haven't you ever stayed awake at night, Babs, wondering what life is all about? Haven't you ever been so lonely you would have gladly traded everything you have to have one friend close enough to share your deepest feelings with? Haven't you ever been let down so badly, even by Phillip, you wondered if life was worth living?" She could see her shot had struck home. "God doesn't let people down. I know that now. He sent His Son to show us the best and only way to live." She broke off. What she said could be crucial at this point. She prayed silently for guidance.

Babs was no longer cynical or laughing. "Then you believe God controls everything in your life and that it's all for a purpose?"

Honor hesitated, choosing her words carefully. "Only when we accept that we are under God's control. So long as we go our way, feeling we are in charge, we step out from under His protection —" She searched for a parable. "If we were walking together down the street under an umbrella and I deliberately chose to step out from under it, I would be subject to the storm."

"But Christians still have storms in their lives." Babs's green eyes were more speculative than antagonistic. "Why doesn't God take better care of those who worship Him?"

For an instant Honor thought of James's lightly asking how she knew it wasn't God's will for her to marry him instead of Phillip. A spasm of regret chased shadows into her eyes. "Sometimes God does send trials, Judge Bell says. I really think, though, that most of the time we bring them to ourselves when we refuse to follow Him."

Babs slowly rose. "Glad I came." So few words in response to the message of salvation. Honor's heart sank as she hesitated, then said, "Babs, it wasn't until after my wedding I stopped rebelling against God and accepted Christ. I can honestly say it's made all the difference in the world. If you want real happiness you will seek God and help Phillip do the same." There! It was out.

Babs looked amazed. "I'd have thought you were —" Her face flushed. "I won't say it. I'll think about it, Honor."

"Don't wait too long." Honor could feel the strain in her voice. "Goodnight, Babs." Prey to her own emotions, Honor still rejoiced. At least some of the bitterness and

177

suspicion Babs carried for her had gone. Would she consider what Honor had said? Troubled by her own flippant remarks to James, desiring to share the Lord she had ignored so long, and concerned over wondering if she could become the kind of witness she wanted to be, she restlessly wandered around her room, then donned her riding habit for the second time that day. Jingles was much better now. Maybe she could either lead him or ride a little on the path near the house.

Cautiously she slipped downstairs and out the door, noting it was ajar. How strange Juan had not locked it as usual! Was someone else prowling? She laughed at her groundless fear. Why get panicky over an unlocked door?

The moon was bright as she walked toward the corral, keeping her head turned back over her shoulder. Why should she feel as if she had been observed slipping from the house? Intent on watching the front door she ran smack into a solid, tall figure in riding clothes.

"Phillip!"

There was slight sound, then the man pushed back his sombrero and grinned sardonically. "Sorry to disappoint you, Mrs. Travis. Not Phillip. Just your husband."

James Travis stood bareheaded before her.

How maddening! Now what would he believe about her? Honor wasn't long in finding out.

"Why did you invite Babs here? As a cover? Seems like you could wait a bit before sneaking out to meet Phillip."

"I did not come out to meet Phillip!"

"Oh?" She could see his lip curl even in the moonlight. "Then what, may I ask, are you doing running around the ranch in the middle of the night?"

Her voice quivered. "Maybe you can't understand how hard it is for me to be here." Mistaking his silence for disbelief, she stumbled on. "How would you like to live in a place where you were watched, mistrusted? How would you like to have someone spying on you all the time, waiting for you to make a mistake?"

"I was not spying. I have every right to be here. I live at Casa del Sol — or haven't you noticed?"

"I've noticed. I've noticed how everyone around here jumps without even asking how high when you speak. Phillip —"

"So you're still in love with him!"

She ignored the savage way he cut the air with his riding crop. "I am not in love with him! That doesn't mean I can't see what you are too blind to notice. Phillip worships you, wishes with all his heart and soul he could be like you! He envies your strength, longs to be able to take control as you do —"

"And covets my wife."

"He does not! You were right. He never loved anyone but Babs. I was a passing fancy, like all the rest." She paused for breath. "I hope Phillip and Babs marry and get as far away from you as possible. You don't know how to love anyone but yourself!"

It was curious what strange tricks moonlight could play. For an instant she could have sworn a shadow of terrible pain crossed the face above her. There was something deadly in his voice as he softly asked, "Oh? Have you so soon forgotten?" She was inexorably being drawn to him. Her cry of protest was smothered by his kiss, gentle at first, then demanding. When he lifted his face from hers she was exhausted.

"Good night, Mrs. Travis." With giant strides he was at the corral. Before Honor could move he had cut out Sol, leaped to his bare back, and had disappeared around the bend in the moonlight.

18

As she had done so many times before, Honor stood by her window, gazing down with unseeing eyes. The autumn leaves that used to greet her were gone. They had been replaced with a soft white mantle that had come during the night. She had seldom seen snow in San Francisco. Even if it did fall, the shining veil soon melted, leaving no trace of its coming. Here it meant stillness beyond belief. Every twig proudly bore its new winter garb, shining in the sun that had come out to beam on the scene.

Two laughing figures ran into view, hand in hand. Babs's scarlet coat was a brilliant spot against the all-white background. Honor smiled in sympathy as Babs's silvery laugh rang out. The change in their red-headed guest in the weeks since she had come to visit Casa del Sol was incredible. And Phillip! Honor couldn't stem the tide of warmth flooding her. Gradually Phillip Travis was growing up after all the years of childish self-indulgence.

"Come on out, Honor!"

She shook her head but called from her

window. "I have something else to do. Maybe later."

"Sissy!" Babs's upturned, laughing face glowed. She snatched a handful of snow and threw it upward as Honor slammed down the window. If only she could be out there with them! If only James — but her husband was more unapproachable than ever. She had thought after the night by the corral things might get better. He was courteous, nothing more. He treated her exactly the way he treated Babs. If he noticed Phillip's and Babs's speculative gazes he ignored them.

Only once had he unbent. Phillip had insisted on being given more responsibility around the ranch. Reluctantly James had assigned him work, and it had been done well. James had sought out Honor.

"I just wanted to say I appreciate your telling me how Phillip feels." His voice was husky. "I believe he and Babs will marry and live on the ranch. I also believe they can be happy here." James had wheeled and left the room before Honor could reply.

"Hey, Honor!" Phillip's call drew her back to the window. He was lugging a huge old-fashioned sled that he must have discovered in the barn. "We're going to the big hill out back. Want to come?"

Honor's determination not to be a third

party weakened. Babs was smiling and beckoning. It was too much. In a spirit of gay recklessness she threw wide her window. "Be right down!" In moments she was bundled into a heavy winter coat James had brought home from a trip to Flagstaff and sent to her by Carlotta. She snuggled in its warmth. Dark green evergreen spires tipped with snow enticed. Why worry on a day like this?

It was the most glorious day she could remember. The snow was perfect, packing down the way it had on sled hills when she was a child. Each time she raced downhill was a thrill. Sometimes alone, or with Babs; sometimes all three of them. The great *whoosh!* across the surface, growing speed, pelting down, and the final slowing and long uphill climb.

"I've never been happier," Babs confided as she and Honor pulled the big sled up the long hill after a particularly exhilarating slide. Her cheeks were redder than her coat, with no need for paint.

"It shows." Honor smiled at the other girl.

"I know." Babs's teeth gleamed. "Phillip asked me last night to marry him — on one condition." Honor could feel herself begin to tense as Babs continued. "He wants to live on the ranch. No more playboy stuff. He certainly has changed since we came here."

"What about you, Babs?"

"Me, too." She grinned impishly at Honor. "Thanks to you. When I saw how much Phillip appreciated your simplicity I decided to take stock of myself. That's why I spent so many hours alone at the South Rim."

Honor scarcely dared breathe. "And?"

"And I decided you weren't for real." She laughed at the disappointment in Honor's face. "Don't look so shocked. That was then. Since I've been here I know it's real. Someday maybe I'll even have you introduce me to your Friend." There was no mistaking her meaning.

Honor's heart swelled. It was worth all the pain and trouble she had gone through to hear Babs say that. "Don't wait too long."

"I won't." Babs twisted the emerald, now worn on her left hand. "I want to talk to Phillip about some things, and —"

"Hurry with the sled, you two! Winter will be over before you get here!" Further confidences were broken, but Babs's warm smile as she broke free and ran the few remaining steps up the hill promised other talks.

184

Honor trudged slowly, filled with her own thoughts. So Babs and Phillip would marry. A flick of pain at the thought of her own shadowy romance brought a lump to her throat, but she pushed it back. Phillip and Babs were arguing when she reached them.

"Aw, Babs, it's nothing. I've gone down that other side a hundred times when I was a kid." He pointed opposite the well-beaten path they had been using to a sharper decline, dotted with green trees.

"You aren't a kid. You don't know what might be under all that snow." Babs looked worried.

"I just want one trip down there."

"Please, Phillip, don't go." Honor added her entreaty to Babs's. "James has warned me so many times of the dangers on the ranch —"

"Dangers!" Phillip drew himself up in a ridiculous pose. "I know this ranch as well as I know my own bedroom." He flung himself to the awkward sled and with his feet pushed the conveyance toward the edge of the bank.

"*Stop!*" The hail came from a tall man running toward them, his face a thundercloud in its command. "Don't push off that sled!"

Honor saw the opposition roused in

Phillip by James's curt order.

"Sorry, brother! I get first ride." With a mighty shove he pushed over the edge and started down before James could reach him. "This is the life!" His voice floated back to them, only to be drowned out. The sled must have hit a hidden snag. For one terrible moment it seemed to stand on end. Phillip was thrown downhill, sliding, arms flailing in a vain effort to stop his momentum. To the horrified gaze of the onlookers he gathered speed in spite of his efforts, smashed into a great tree, and crumpled into a heap.

"Phillip!" Heedless of his own safety, James started down the hill. His great boots sank into the snow as he went, leaving giant stride marks. Clutching at every outstretched branch, he slipped, slid, and by sheer determination stopped where Phillip lay horribly crumpled.

Babs was the first to come to her senses. "Quick! We'll get help!" She grabbed Honor's arm, shaking her back to reality. "We've got to get back to the house and call a doctor. Or at least get Juan and Rosa. They'll know what to do." Cupping her hands around her mouth she called to James, "We're going for help."

Fear lent wings to their feet as they raced

back to the house. They burst into the kitchen. "Rosa, Phillip's hurt. Where's Juan?"

Concern didn't detract from Rosa's swift actions. "Out shoveling." She threw open the door and called to him, waving her arms imperatively. "Juan! Quickly, Felipe is hurt!"

In moments Juan, Babs, and Honor were huddled in the big Willys as it churned through the snow down a little-used road that would bring them out only a few hundred feet below the brothers. "I'm so thankful for this heavy car," Honor breathed.

Juan braked, stopped, and was out of the car and up the separating distance, closely followed by the two girls. James looked up to answer the unspoken question trembling on their lips. "He's hurt — badly." He pressed his scarf against Phillip's head. Honor could see bright bloodstains on the snow. "We've got to get him to a doctor."

"Rosa is calling one now." Honor found her voice, but James shook his head. "We can't wait for a doctor. We'll take him to Flagstaff immediately."

Honor's involuntary protest died under the look of anguish in James's eyes. "But how —" she faltered.

"The roads are clear." Already Juan and James were lifting Phillip carefully, inching their way down to the car. "We'll get him in the back where he can lie down. Mama Rosa will know what to do until we get to Flag-staff."

It was a nightmare Honor would never forget. The seemingly endless procession to the house, the fitting in all of them and still leaving room for Phillip to half lie down.

"Can you drive?" James whirled toward Honor. "I want Juan to help me steady Phillip."

"Not in snow and ice." She shivered. "I only learned here this fall."

"I can." Babs's lips were white but deter-mined. Already she was slipping into the driver's seat. Mama Rosa stayed with the two men, pressing compresses hard on the wound spurting blood. Carlotta huddled between Babs and Honor in the front seat. There had been no question but that they would all go. *It's a family,* Honor thought. *My family.* But there was no time to explore such thoughts.

The road to Flagstaff was icy and had not been sanded. In spite of Babs's skillful han-dling of the car, it still slid now and then.

Once Babs looked across at Honor. "Now's the time to call on that God you told me about." There was no mockery in her words.

"I am." Honor's lips moved silently.

Mile after mile they traveled as fast as Babs dared. When they reached the outskirts of Flagstaff, Honor breathed normally again, but it wasn't until they were in the emergency waiting room with Phillip on his way to surgery that some of the tenseness left her.

"He's cut badly on his head," the doctor had told them after the first cursory examination. "He doesn't appear to have lost too much blood. No bones appear to be broken but —" he hesitated "— there is always the danger of internal bleeding."

If James Travis's face could have gone whiter it did. Balm stifled a little moan, and Honor reached for her hand to grip it hard. "Don't, Babs. God will take care of Phillip. I know He will." Something in her level look steadied Babs, who clung to her.

But James couldn't hold back bitter words. "If there really is a God, why did He let Phillip get hurt in the first place?"

Honor's heart sank. James would never understand. "God didn't force Phillip to go down that hill." James didn't speak but turned away, leaving Honor shaken. In spite of everything, she had hoped they could make their marriage work. But if James had no use for God, how could it ever be?

It seemed hours before the doctor returned. His face was grave. "He will live." His words were almost lost in the gasps of relief, but the doctor's face didn't lighten. "He will live, but —" He looked around the little group, at James last of all. "The head wound is close to his eyes. We found a piece of bone depressed into the brain. The surgeons are working with it now. Until it is over and he wakens we just won't know."

"Just won't know what?" James's face blazed.

The doctor's face wrinkled in sympathy. "Whether he will ever see again."

Honor felt the shock ripple around the circle.

"Blind!" James repeated stupidly.

"There is that possibility." The doctor gripped James's arm. "We are doing everything humanly possible, and —"

"You said humanly possible. What else could be done?" James's ashen face frightened Honor.

The doctor didn't waver. "There is a power higher than man." With another strong pressure on James's arm, he turned and left them. This time there was no mockery in James's voice. "Honor?" He turned toward her, stumbling a bit. "Honor? You know that higher power. Will you do something?" The pleading in his eyes hurt Honor.

"I have been praying ever since the accident."

Babs seemed to come to life. "Honor, if I promised God to live as He wants, would He save Phillip's sight?"

Honor's lips fell stiff. "You can't bargain with God. All we can do is pray — and wait."

"She's right." Judge Bell stood in the doorway, panting as if he had been running. Babs instinctively turned toward the kindness in his face.

"There, lassie, we must trust our Father in heaven —"

"Trust Him! I don't even know Him!" James's face contorted in agony. "All this time, you tried to tell me, and I wouldn't listen. Daddy — is Phillip's accident a punishment because I haven't believed?"

Honor stood rooted in sorrow. She remembered asking the same question.

"No." There was something magnificent about the judge. "God punishes us for our own sins, not those of others."

James's face was chalky. He went on as if he had not heard. "I should have been an example. Why haven't I been what I should have been? Phillip is weak, and I knew it." He raised dull eyes toward Honor. "If I had believed in Christ and told Phillip how important it was, maybe he wouldn't be such a mess. Maybe he wouldn't even be lying there now." His harsh laugh grated in the shocked silence. "I contributed to his weakness."

Honor could not bear his suffering. She turned away.

James looked at Daddy Bell. "You told me I would have to face God, to answer for laughing at the idea I wasn't in total control. But did it have to come this way? Did anyone ever sin as I have, deliberately choosing to ignore everything that really matters in life?"

"Come, laddie." Daddy Bell placed his arm around James as if he had been a child. "We'll fight this out together."

Honor and Babs stood frozen as the two men, one bent with the ministry of years, the other from his growing recognition of sin and careless ignorance of sacred things, slowly walked down the long hall and disappeared behind a door marked CHAPEL.

Honor could not speak. Even when Babs moaned and sank into a chair, Honor remained standing straight, looking down the hall. It suddenly seemed a great gulf separating her from James. What happened now would literally save her husband's life or leave him empty, unfulfilled, bitter.

"Oh, God, let him accept Your Son that he might be forgiven." It was all she could whisper. If only she could be at his side! She could not. It would be for Judge Bell to make clear the only path that did not lead to spiritual death. Then James must make the decision, not to attempt a bargain with God for his brother's sight, but to seal himself as God's child, forgiven and willing to obey.

Was all of life a fight? Sickness, health — good, evil — God, Satan — in spite of her studies the thoughts left Honor helpless.

What was happening in the little chapel? Was James listening with his heart instead of with his head, as so many educated minds seemed to do? Could the prejudices and false images he had built be shattered? Yes! Hadn't God done exactly that for her?

A little cry from Babs snapped Honor from her trancelike state. There was work to do here. God would help James. She would cling to that hope and silently pray. Her other prayers for Phillip and Babs mingled together in one great plea to God.

For hours she and Babs sat together. The

waiting room was mercifully empty of others. Only fear kept them company, and after a time, even it was blunted by sheer exhaustion. At first Honor tried to keep up a conversation with Babs, but it was useless. Babs's eyes were fixed on the door to the emergency room. Was she remembering all the laughing days they had spent carelessly going their pleasure-mad way? Was she remembering moments at the canyon when she had gone away from the others to evaluate? Or was she even remembering days long ago before Phillip, days when she said she had gone to Sunday school?

Honor's brain whirled. The broken woman next to her was a far cry from the worldly creature who had once infuriated a rebellious girl by telling her the truth about Phillip. Impulsively Honor laid her hand over Babs's clenched ones.

The green eyes swung to her briefly. A small tremor of her lips betrayed tightly held emotion, and her hands opened to clasp the one extended in friendship. There was a gentle pressure of the cold fingers that slowly warmed, then the icy face gave way to pain, unashamed.

An eon of time seemed to have passed before the chapel door swung open. Honor held her breath. What would be the results of what had happened in the little room?

"James has found his God." Daddy's tired face still radiated.

With a little cry Honor ran to them. "It wasn't just to save Phillip?"

James went white to the lips, and Honor wished fervently she had bitten her tongue to hold back the words.

"No. It wasn't for Phillip." He looked past her, eyes dulled instead of expectant as they had been before. "I read your Bible, Honor. At first, it was with scorn. How could anyone believe any tale so simple?" His dark eyes were almost black in their intensity. "You had circled a place." He fumbled in the Bible she knew so well, found the marked passage. "John three sixteen: 'For God so loved the world, that he gave his only begotten Son, that whosoever believeth in him should not perish, but have everlasting life.' " He closed the Book, almost reverently. "I still wouldn't admit the feeling I had when I read it." A spasm of pain crossed his face. "Daddy Bell made me reread it. Then I knew. *Whosoever* meant me, and everyone. Every man, woman, and child on earth must bow before God, admit they are sinners, and realize the fact of the Lord Jesus Christ's death in their place so that they might have forgiveness, mercy, salvation. I only wish I had listened and accepted it all years ago." The last words were almost a whisper.

For an ecstatic moment Honor felt faint from joy and relief. Her prayers had been answered — James was saved! Now there was nothing to stand between them! Now they could — the thought died. Just because James had accepted Christ didn't mean he loved the woman he'd married under such bizarre circumstances.

"I intend to set straight everything I have done to wrong others." James's voice broke into her mind.

Honor bit her lip. He must mean her. He would feel the only way to make things right was to release her. Could she stand the pain still ahead? Would she never stop paying for her rebellion and willfulness, even though she was forgiven?

And James — he would carry forever the memory of the way he had married his twin's fiancée in an underhanded way. Both would pay in being freed by law from unfulfilled vows, bound in God's sight — and in their own. Granny's warning, Keith's pleadings — all had led to this, and there was no one to blame but herself.

She breathed raggedly. It was not the time to explore their relationship, with Phillip

196

still in danger, nor was it in days following. Babs haunted the hospital. For even though the doctors were hopeful, there was nothing to do but wait.

11

One thing that came about from all the trouble was a new closeness between Babs and Honor. From distrust to wariness, as last to the acceptance of Honor's hand at the hospital that terrible night, Babs took slow steps toward trusting another woman. Honor sensed the struggle. How terrible to have lived among those where self-preservation ruled out real friendship!

One evening Babs said, "Honor, the hardest thing in the world for me is to admit I'm wrong, but if I'd admitted to myself at the canyon what I knew you were, I'd never have said all those terrible things."

Honor looked up from mending a blouse she'd brought to the hospital. "They were all true. I didn't realize how true until I came here and accepted Christ. I'm glad you said what you did, although it made me angry. Even though I couldn't accept it at the time, I thought of it later and admitted you were right."

"Even if Phillip is blind, I'm going to marry him."

Honor dropped her mending. "Will he?"

"I'm not letting him go again — ever."

There was nothing of the sophisticate in the determination in Babs's face. "It's not from pity. I've always loved him. I just couldn't trust him not to find another pretty face, and now he may not be able to even see those faces."

"Stop it!" Honor dropped the blouse and shook Babs hard. "The doctor says he has every reason to believe Phillip will be all right."

"Then why doesn't he regain total consciousness?" The cry echoed doubts in Honor's own mind. "Honor, I have to have something to hang on to, like you have. Would God really forgive me and send peace?"

"If you confess yourself a sinner."

"You'll never know how great a sinner." The admission was low.

"I don't want to. It's between you and God. That's why Jesus died on the cross, to save you forever from all that. He took your place, Babs."

"But what do I do?"

"Just repent and then accept it. Salvation is a free gift. You gain eternal life. You gain Christ and the Holy Spirit and peace from God. You are free, Babs, free from every ugly thing in your past." Honor breathed a prayer and took Babs's ice-cold hands in her own. "Just tell Him you are sorry for all your sins and accept the gift of His Son and salvation."

"I —" The opening of the door from Phillip's room cut her short.

"He is awake." The doctor's smile warmed Honor's heart.

Babs remained frozen in place for one second, then gave a low cry and ran into the room.

"It's all right," the doctor told Honor. "The first thing he said was, 'Where's Babs?' "

Babs didn't stay long in Phillip's room. When she came back she was radiant. "He complained of a headache, but he can see!"

Honor felt as if the strain that had been holding her up suddenly gave way. She stumbled into a chair, trying to form words for the praise and gladness in her heart. Phillip would not be blind! *Please,* her heart whispered, *cure Phillip and Babs of a different kind of blindness and help them find You.* What would Babs have said if the door had not opened just when it did? She had been close, so close!

The question haunted Honor for the next week. During that week Phillip was pronounced fit and sent home. What a far cry from that terrible trip they had made taking him to the hospital!

The touring car with James, Honor, Phillip, and Babs swung into the driveway to be greeted with Christmas garnish. Decorations were everywhere. The Hernandez family had spread sweet-smelling boughs, bright ribbons, every kind of decoration they could imagine.

"Some welcome home." Phillip sounded subdued. "I could have been —"

"Thank God you aren't." James spoke softly.

"You? Thanking God?"

But the old, mocking light died from Phillip's face as James replied, "I have discovered what a fool I have been in discounting the only thing in the world that really matters."

Phillip swung to Babs, standing close in the lightly falling snow. "I suppose next you'll be telling me you feel the same."

Honor's fingers clenched until they were white, even under their warm wool mitten covering. The group of four stood motionless. Could Babs sense she was at a crossroads?

"I —" her pleading gaze at Honor lifted to Phillip's handsome face "— I am glad to be home." She broke free of the group and hurried through the massive front door.

Honor's disappointment spilled over. She had to turn away from the two men to hide her telltale face. Babs had been so close! It was all she could do to pretend gaiety at the Mexican meal Rosa and Carlotta had prepared to welcome Phillip home. Once she met James's searching eyes, and a faltering smile hovered on her lips. Later he whispered, "Don't forget — God reached even me."

In the library before the fire after dinner Phillip paced restlessly and finally whirled toward Babs. "Well, are you going to marry me on Christmas Eve?"

Babs gasped, then recovered something of her old haughtiness. "I am not." Before anyone could move she added, "But I will marry you on Christmas Day."

"This is our cue for an exit." James motioned Honor out of the room.

"Well, it looks as if things are going to work out for Phillip and Babs." Honor stopped at the foot of the great staircase and smiled at James.

His face didn't light up the way she had expected. For one moment he seemed to be looking over her head and into the future. Somber, brooding, his answer chilled her. "Yes, things have turned out for them. But what about us?"

Before she could speak, he was gone.

As she slowly mounted the stairs to her room, again she fell alone — only this time God was there to help her bear the pain. Yet even that pain gave way before another disappointment the same night. After tossing and turning for what seemed like hours she was startled to hear her door slowly opening.

"Honor?" Babs glided to the bed.

"Babs!" Surprise choked off Honor's voice. "Are you ill?"

"No."

The snow outside had stopped earlier. Now a pale moon targeted the red-haired woman through Honor's partly uncurtained window. Yet even the dim light failed to hide her agitation. Her hands were icy as one brushed against Honor's face.

"Honor? I have to talk with you."

Sleep fled. "What is wrong, Babs?"

"I tried to tell Phillip what you said about God."

"And?" Honor held her breath.

"He laughed. Not so much as he would have done before the accident, but he still laughed."

Honor's heart ached for the desolate sound in her friend's voice. "What about you, Babs? You know it's all true, don't you?"

"Yes." Babs's face turned even paler. "But I can't accept it." As if she felt Honor's shock she brokenly added, "I've waited years for Phillip to notice me in a real way. Nothing must spoil that!"

Her cry echoed in Honor's heart, a duplicate of her own cry at the canyon's edge what seemed like eons ago. "You are choosing Phillip instead of God?"

"I must." The icy hands clutched the warm one Honor held out. "Phillip has already changed more than I ever thought possible. We're going to make our home here. He's going to give up drinking and all that. Isn't it enough?" Her voice was anguished.

"No, Babs." The inflexibility of the two words wilted Babs.

Honor couldn't keep despair from her voice as she cried out, "The greatest sin in the world is not accepting the free gift of salvation through the Lord Jesus Christ. All the being good in the world, all the good deeds won't save you or anyone. Please, Babs." Her voice rose. "Don't turn your back on Him. Don't crucify the Lord again by your refusal to accept Him!"

Babs slowly withdrew her hands from Honor's desperate clutch. Her eyes held fear, regret, pain. She rose from the bed where she'd been seated to tower over Honor. "I have no choice. I can never give up Phillip."

For one wild moment Honor wondered — should she tell Babs she, too, had once made that same choice and with what tragic results? Slowly she shook her head. Now was not the time for that. Instead she said, "Babs, I once demanded my own way and have gone through agony because of it. I had to come to Christ just as I would have done before. But instead of it being easy and natural, there were years of pain and bitterness in between. We have to learn the same lessons, whether we do it God's way — or our own, and our way is hard."

"Someday, if Phillip can accept — I will, too." Babs slipped out.

The tears on Honor's pillow that night were not for herself.

Christmas and the wedding rushed toward them. Soon it was Christmas Eve. Babs had not mentioned her decision since that night. Neither had Honor, who now lay sleepless. When God directed her to speak she would. Until then, she could only pray.

At least she could be thankful for the change in Phillip. He was becoming more like his brother every day. He had accepted his future at Casa del Sol, relishing it. The brothers spent time planning how to make it more efficient. Phillip had come up with some surprisingly good ideas. "Just because I wasn't running this place doesn't mean I never thought about it." The casual remark didn't hide his pleasure at their compliments.

Suddenly Honor could stand the confines of her room no longer. James's inscrutable eyes watched her from every corner. She would slip down to the library and find something to read. James still had her Bible, but she had noticed a big one downstairs with more references than the small one Daddy Bell had given her.

Before she could reconsider, Honor thrust her arms into a heavy turquoise quilted robe and matching slippers. She ran lightly down the stairs, struggled with the heavy doors, then crept inside. Fumbling for the light switch, she was immobilized by the tall, dark figure rising from the couch, etched against glowing flames in the fireplace.

"James?"

"At least you didn't call me Phillip. Do come into my parlor, dear little fly."

Why did he still have the power to hurt her? Or was it weariness in his voice instead of sarcasm? She ran her hand lightly over her hair. "I couldn't sleep. I came for a book."

He came a step nearer. "And just why couldn't you sleep?"

She could feel it coming — the floods of feeling behind the dam of control she had built so carefully. If she answered, that last line of defense would crumble under the onslaught.

"I asked why you couldn't sleep."

His insistence was the final undoing. "How could you expect me to sleep — under the circumstances?"

"You mean because Phillip is marrying Babs tomorrow?" She had never felt as flayed as she did by his accusation.

"Don't be completely stupid!" She hadn't known she could blaze so. All the long nights of wondering, of loving him hopelessly burst forth. "It's you, James Travis. Are you too insane to see it?"

A disbelieving look crept over his face. "Just what is that supposed to mean?"

The ice in his voice drowned all determination to tell him the truth. Honor fell back on the old, original reason. "You really think any woman in my position could be happy, married to a man who did it to protect her from his own brother?" She could feel his scrutiny even when she dropped her eyes to study the pattern one nervous, slippered foot was making on the floor.

"Oh, that." His voice went lifeless. For a moment he turned to the fire. The lights from the Christmas tree shone on his face, softening it into vulnerability. Honor knew she would never forget the way he looked. To hide the weakness threatening to paralyze her, she walked to the window, noting the heavy frost patterns and that it had begun to snow again.

"Honor, would you come sit down, please." There was no spark in the request. Slowly she turned and crossed to the fire, carefully avoiding him.

"Honor, when I was in the chapel at the hospital and finally quit trying to outrun God, I made a promise." Something in the gravity of his tone chilled her. "You had said people couldn't bargain with God. I didn't. I did tell Him that when it was all over I'd do what I could to make up to you for marrying you."

For one wild moment Honor's heart leaped. Did he mean that he had learned to care? She was frozen anew by his next words. Face half in shadow, he poked the fire again. "I have put it off, hoping something would happen to change things.

Maybe I was even hoping for a miracle. I planned to wait until after the wedding tomorrow." He threw the poker down with a little crash. "I can't wait any longer."

In spite of the warm room Honor shivered with premonition. Could God hear the silent prayer unconsciously going up for help?

"I can't go on the way things are. It's too hard having you here, knowing you despise me."

Shocked, she opened her mouth to protest, only to have the words die on her lips as he said, "I want you to go away. The day after the wedding I'll take you to Flagstaff. We can get the marriage annulled. I'll settle enough finances on you so you can be independent, but I won't keep you here any longer."

Sheer fury overrode Honor's sense of loss. Very slowly she rose to her feet, glaring up at the man who was her husband yet was not her husband. "So now that you've married me, you'll just pack me off the way you'd discard an old pair of shoes." She failed to understand what was in James's eyes. "Well, let me tell you something, Mr. Travis. I won't be shipped off and have money settled on me! I'm not leaving Casa del Sol. You don't have to like it, but you married me for better or for worse. I'm legally your wife. There's nothing you can do about it unless you want the whole story spread across the front page of every newspaper in Arizona."

She paused for breath, then went on. "Have you ever once considered that I don't want to go?"

"I have considered it." His face was still in shadow, but the words came out individually, like small, hard ice cubes hitting a tile floor. "I know you would rather live in misery than break a promise. Now that I have stopped running from God I appreciate it even more. But the promise you made was made falsely. I can't hold you to it."

"So you intend to dispose of me quite properly."

For one moment she felt she had gone too far. There was a quick flash in the set face. "I told you. I can't go on like we are now." In one stride he came close, gripping her by the shoulders, forcing her to look up at him. "If you stay at Casa del Sol it can no longer be as a guest, Honor Travis. It will be as my wife, living with me in holy matrimony the way God intended man and woman to live." His look seared her very soul. "Will you stay under those circumstances? Or will you go to Flagstaff day after tomorrow, as I suggested?"

Honor's knees felt weak. "You mean — you mean you want me to stay as your wife?"

"Want you! I have wanted you since the day I looked up to see you standing in the hall of my home." His grip tightened. "If ever a man wanted a woman, I want you. You have brought sunlight and laughter. You have brought healing between Phillip and me. You have brought everything a man could ever want. Most of all, you have brought God into this house." His voice had dropped almost to a whisper. "Yes, I want you here — but not as a guest."

Honor was speechless, shaken by his passion. "Then all the time — even when you married me — it wasn't just because you pitied me?"

"No, Honor. It was because I loved you. I didn't know it myself at first. I tried to tell myself it was to save you from Phillip. It wasn't. I fell in love with you the day you came."

Honor's senses were reeling. "But — the day we were married, when I said you probably would say you'd fallen in love with me —" her voice failed.

"Would you have believed me?"

"Not then."

"And now?" The clock ticked off seconds, repeating his question: *And now? And now?*

She was not quite ready to give in. "You said friends are people who trusted you." She moistened her suddenly dry lips. "You said —"

An amused look cut off her stumbling speech. "I said a lot of things — some in self-defense. What I am telling you now is the truth. I love you, Honor, as I have never loved any other woman. I will never love anyone else, even if you go away."

"Then I had better stay."

"You know my conditions."

"I know."

But James wasn't satisfied. He held her off at arms' length. "Are you staying because you promised — because you don't want to break vows you consider holy, even taken under the circumstances ours were made? Or is it possible that Phillip was right?"

It was becoming increasingly difficult for her to meet his searching gaze. "I don't know what Phillip said."

"Phillip told me weeks ago you had never loved him. You had fallen in love with what you thought he was."

Honor didn't answer. Her mind flashed back to the canyon; her rationalizing what

Phillip might someday be; her determination to cling to him even at the expense of her own relationship with God.

"Well?"

Her eyes grew soft, but she bravely faced him. "Phillip was right." She hurried on, disturbed by the light filling his dark face. "Carlotta asked me which man I loved — you heard her — and my answer."

Color crept into James's face. "It is the only hope I had these past weeks."

Honor wasn't finished. Her clear eyes confirmed her truthfulness. "I was attracted to Phillip, you know that. In San Francisco, at the canyon.

"When I came to Casa del Sol, I had to revamp my opinion. Where was the charming, idle man I knew? My fiance was no longer the laughing Phillip Travis, but 'Senor' — admired, respected, a big man doing a big job. It was hard to put the two together!

"James, I ran ahead of God, went on with the wedding, hoped for the best." Her throat was thick with unshed tears. "I have paid. Learning to know you, feeling I was a duty —" She felt heat creep into her cheeks. "But at least God didn't allow me to actually marry the wrong man."

She faltered as James gently pulled her

closer. "You really care, Honor? You aren't just bound by your vows?"

A flash of mischief crossed her face. "All my childhood heroes rode white horses, just as you do." The hope and disbelief warring in his face were too much. She discarded her pretense. "I am bound, but not only by my vows. I am bound by the love I have for you — love that is second only to my love for the Lord."

Somewhere in the hall the clock struck twelve. Christmas Eve was over; Christmas Day had begun.

Honor closed her eyes and crept closer in her husband's arms, feeling the solid strength of James Travis. For one magnificent moment she seemed to see down the aisle of years — laughing, weeping, loving, sharing, together — loving life with Christ the Son as head of Casa del Sol.